MY BIG FAT ZOMBIE GOLDFISH

JURASSIC CARP

MO O'HARA

ILLUSTRATED BY MAREK JAGUCKI

MACMILLAN CHILDREN'S BOOKS

First published 2015 by Macmillan Children's Books
an imprint of Pan Macmillan
20 New Wharf Road, London N1 9RR
Associated companies throughout the world
www.panmacmillan.com

ISBN 978-1-4472-6383-8

Text copyright © Mo O'Hara 2015
Illustrations copyright © Marek Jagucki 2015

The right of Mo O'Hara and Marek Jagucki to be identified as the
author and illustrator of this work has been asserted by them in
accordance with the Copyright, Designs and Patents Act 1988.

1 3 5 7 9 8 6 4 2

A CIP catalogue record for this book is available from
the British Library.

Printed and bound by CPI Group (UK) Ltd, Croydon CR0 4YY

MY BIG FAT

ZOMBIE

GOLDFISH

JURASSIC CARP

Mo O'Hara grew up in Pennsylvania, USA, but now lives in south-east London. She began her writing and acting career by touring theatres and schools across the UK and Ireland, working as a storyteller. As well as writing books for children Mo has written comedy sketches for Radio 4 and performed her own material in London and Edinburgh. Mo and her big brother once brought their own pet goldfish back from the brink of death.

Quotes from My Big Fat Zombie Goldfish *readers*

'This Franktastic story was so much fun it blew my socks off!' **Sharif (aged 8)**

'I wish I had a swishy fishy!' **Robin (aged 7)**

'Don't look at Frankie! He'll zombify you and you won't be able to stop reading!' **Adil (aged 8)**

'*My Big Fat Zombie Goldfish* is a zombitastic book you won't be able to put down' **Leon (aged 9)**

'It's really funny and Frankie makes me laugh lots' **Spike (aged 7)**

'It was awesome. I read all day when I got it and I couldn't put it down until I was finished' **Becky (aged nearly 9)**

To my best friend Jaimie.

I write about best friends because I have you.

THE
NIGHT KNIGHT

CHAPTER 1
OUR TALE BEGINNETH

Trumpets blared on either side of the school coach as it bumped along the track up to Castlerock Castle. And I don't mean ordinary trumpets. I mean those extra-long pointy ones with flags hanging off them, like you see in wizard-and-dungeon video games.

'Wow, they really went all out for this medieval day!' I said, turning to my best friend Pradeep who was hunched on the seat behind me.

'Bleugh!' he groaned as he filled another sick bag. 'Nice trumpets.'

Pradeep and I usually sit together because

his travel sickness doesn't bug me, but today *he* wouldn't sit next to *me*. You see . . . each class had to dress up as something different for this medieval reconstruction thing – and our class had to dress as peasants.

Top Five Reasons why Dressing as a Peasant is the Best Costume Ever:
1) You're *SUPPOSED* to be messy and covered in dirt. Brilliant!
2) If your peasant outfit is too clean, you *have* to jump in puddles to make it muddy.
3) You get to wear tights (which are surprisingly comfortable for climbing trees).
4) Mum couldn't say: 'There's no way you can go to school looking like that!' because I *COULD*.
5) You can make mud out of perfectly dry dirt, just to jump in it!

Frankie, my big fat zombie goldfish, had enjoyed the whole splashing-in-muddy-puddles thing

too. I unscrewed the
top of the flagon
hanging over
my shoulder
so he could
see out.

'That's
Castlerock
Castle,' I said.
'Looks cool,
huh?'

Frankie shrugged like he wasn't impressed, but
then he caught sight of the moat. He squeezed
out of the top of the flagon and slapped himself
against the window before plopping back with a
muddy splash.

'Frankie, I'm not supposed to get my peasant
costume dirty!' Pradeep groaned from behind us.
His mum hadn't understood the whole 'peasant'
look and sent him to school in a spotless cream
tunic, matching felt cap with a white feather,

and cream tights. He looked a bit like a medieval Milky Bar kid actually. *This* is why he wouldn't sit next to me.

'Hang on,' I said. 'Aren't you going to tell me off for bringing Frankie on a school trip? Or at least remind me that every time I do bring him we end up getting into trouble?'

'No!' mumbled Pradeep as he filled another sick bag. He really must have been feeling ill.

Just then the bus pulled up next to the castle. A man with jingly bells on a very silly-looking hat tapped on the bus driver's widow with a stick with matching jingly bells on it. 'Good morrow, good sir, and bountiful blessings on this glorious day. My name is Archibald of Ditherington.' He jingled as he bowed. 'But you may refer to me as Motley Fool.'

'Isn't that a rock band?' the driver asked.

'Forsooth, you jest!' Motley Fool said with a jingly shake of his stick. 'Do you bringeth the peasants of the town?'

'Huh?' said the bus driver.

The fool cleared his throat. 'It matters not. Beckon the young folk to make haste to the castle, then parketh your cart yonder.' He jingled his stick more curtly in the direction of the car park.

'You what?' the bus driver asked.

Motley took a deep breath. 'Get the kids off the bus then park over there.'

'Oh, right!' The bus driver nodded and then shouted back to us, 'Off here! And don't leave anything on the bus!'

He looked directly at Pradeep as he said that last bit.

CHAPTER 2
HAVE A PEASANT DAY

Pradeep and I picked up his sick bags and got off the bus. We found a bin and then lined up to be counted in by the teachers. Ever since a kid got left behind on a crisp factory tour, they've been extra careful. He got through five mega-bags before anyone found him. I think the school had to pay.

Our teacher Mrs Richards addressed the class. 'I for one am excited about the educational and historically pertinent day that we are about to have.' She was smiling more than I have ever seen a history teacher smile. I guess that's cos they mostly teach us about wars and plagues and stuff. 'Now make sure you pay attention to our guide for the day.'

'Hear ye, hear ye, all you who come to visit Castlerock Castle,' Motley Fool cried. 'Hark and I will tell ye what adventures we have in store.' He waved his jingly stick as he spoke. 'We will witness the three challenges of the Tournament of Castlerock. First, archery, where the knights' accuracy will be tested. Then the boulder lift, in order to judgeth their strength. And finally the joust – to test each knight's ultimate bravery.'

'I can't wait to see the archery!' Pradeep whispered.

'Me too,' I said. 'Plus it'll be great to have a day out for once that has absolutely nothing "evil" about it.'

The words had not even completely left my mouth when we heard the laugh. 'Mwhaaa haa haaa haa haa!'

Then we saw him. My Evil Scientist big brother Mark was dressed in a thick velvet embroidered coat and big baggy velvet shorts. He had dark tights and pointy shoes and was striding towards our class with other kids from his school. They were all wearing fancy clothes and floppy hats.

Motley Fool bowed to them as they approached the drawbridge. 'Good morrow, Lords and Ladies of the Castle. The peasants have arrived to work in the castle yard.'

Mark smiled his creepiest smile. 'Cool . . . um . . . I mean, *cooleth.*'

My flagon started to rattle from side to side as Frankie started trying to escape. Frankie and

Mark have been mortal enemies ever since Mark dunked him in toxic gunge and tried to flush him.

'Shhh, Frankie!' I whispered.

'Today, we are role-playing daily life in the medieval world,' Mrs Richards called to our class. 'So, the wishes of the Lords and Ladies, *within reason* –' she stared at Mark as she said that bit – 'are your commands. Peasants, let's head into the castle.'

'Urgh!' Mark stopped just before he stepped on to the drawbridge. 'I can't walk through this muddy puddle. PEASANT!' he shouted.

Motley Fool motioned for Pradeep and me to go and help him.

Throwing my flagon over my shoulder to keep Frankie as far away from Mark as possible, we linked arms to make a seat and lift Mark across the puddle. Just as we were putting him down – Mark's foot kicked back and splashed mud across us both.

'Yuck!' Pradeep groaned, wiping mud from his face and tunic.

'Sorry about that.' Mark smiled. 'My foot must have slipped. Mwhaa haa haa haa haa!'

He strode on ahead with the rest of the Lords and Ladies, and our class of peasants followed.

Frankie was thrashing hard in his flagon now and pushing at the opening. I popped open the cork to let him see that Mark was gone.

'At least Mark didn't realize that Frankie's here,' I said to Pradeep. 'And there's no sign of Fang, Mark's evil vampire kitten. We can still have a fun day. We just need to make sure that we avoid Mark.'

'Right! I mean, it could be worse!' Pradeep joked. 'My Evil Computer Genius big brother Sanj could be here too.'

That's when we heard an evil wheeze.

CHAPTER 3
EVIL LOOKETH AS EVIL DOETH

'You have got to be kidding me!' I said.

Dressed in a full medieval wizard's outfit, Sanj, Pradeep's Evil Computer Genius big brother, strode towards us from the castle.

'Nice hat,' Pradeep said as I popped the cork back into Frankie's flagon so he couldn't fling himself out at Sanj.

'I thought the outfit was appropriate as I am a computing wizard.' Sanj smiled his creepy smile. 'My gifted and talented school was asked to participate and we were all given special costumes that befitted our talents.' He looked at our grimy peasant outfits. 'As were

you.' He wheezed his evil laugh and leaned
closer.

Suddenly
the cork, and
Frankie, popped
out of the top of
the flagon and
shot straight at
Sanj, thwacking
him square on the
nose.

'Argh!' Sanj shouted as he flailed his wand
blindly.

'Frankie, stop!' I yelled, pulling the zombie
goldfish off Sanj's nose and shoving him back
into the flagon.

'Nnnnny nnnose!' Sanj said in a way that
sounded like he had a dozen cotton balls shoved
up there. 'Naaal nnnnet nnnoou for nnisss . . .
fnnnish!'

'I'm sorry?' I asked.

'I think he said, "I'll get you for this . . . dish!"'
Pradeep said.

'Urgh!' Sanj shouted. 'Fnnish! Fnnishh!'

'Oh, *fish*,' Pradeep and I said at the same time.

'Ni nnate nnat fnnnish!' Sanj mumbled and
stormed back towards the castle.

'Oh no,' I said. 'He'll tell Mark about Frankie
and that's going to mean trouble.'

'Not if we stay out of their way,' reasoned
Pradeep.

Just then the trumpets sounded again.

'That's the signal for the start of the archery,
Tom!' Pradeep cried. 'Let's get in there before we
miss it!'

We ran over the drawbridge, but the courtyard
was so crowded that we couldn't see the knights.
Pradeep pointed at one of the low castle walls. It
was thick and sturdy and had special cut-out bits
where *I think* they used to put archers or cannons
during battles. They were like ready-made seats
for the contest.

'Good idea,' I said. 'We'll see perfectly from up there.'

I hung Frankie's flagon around my neck and we climbed some wooden ladders that were leaning against the wall.

As we looked down into the courtyard we could see a mass of peasants. The Lords and Ladies of Mark's school and the gifted and talented wizards, soothsayers, Kings and Queens from Sanj's school were all seated on a platforms around the fenced-off tournament area. Then we saw the knights. Their suits of armour glimmered in the sun as they stood in a row. Quivers of arrows hung by their sides and long heavy bows were in their hands. I uncorked Frankie's flagon so he could see too.

Motley Fool stepped out in front of the crowd. He pointed to the targets that were lined up against the castle wall. 'Good morrow and welcome, Ladies, Lords and castle folk. Herewith begins the first of our three events! Whomsoever striketh the target most exactly shall taketh the victory.'

One of the peasants shouted, 'What?'

Motley Fool added, 'The best shot winneth the contest!'

Everyone cheered again. I spotted Mark in the stands. He and Sanj were whispering together and looking over at the knights.

'Let us introduceth our noble knights!' Motley Fool shouted, and jingled his stick. A knight in silver armour with a picture of a red rose, wrapped around a sword, on his chest stepped forward.

'The Knight of the Rose!' cried Motley. The knight bowed and everyone clapped.

Frankie peeked out of his flagon but didn't seem impressed.

Next, a knight wearing a golden suit of

armour and a helmet like a pointy crown
stepped forward. 'The Knight of the Crown!'
Jingled Motley Fool. He too bowed and everyone
cheered.

Frankie yawned.

'Don't be rude, Frankie,' Pradeep said. 'You
couldn't do what they're doing, could you?'

Frankie glared at Pradeep, flipped out of the
flagon and on to the wall. He scooped up several
pebbles in his mouth and then shuffled around
so he was facing one of the trumpets at the side
of the tournament area. With a series of pops, he
shot the pebbles out of his mouth. Every single
one pinged off the end of the brass trumpet,
sounding like a machine-gun splatter of tiny bells.

Frankie wiped his fins, looked at us with a look
that said, 'And you were saying?' and jumped
back into the flagon.

CHAPTER 4
ON TARGET FOR EVIL

'OK, that was pretty impressive,' mumbled Pradeep, as the third knight stepped forward. He was wearing silver armour and had a white horse on his chest plate and shield.

'Please welcometh . . . the Knight-Mare!' Motley Fool shouted and the crowd groaned. The Knight-Mare bowed, but I swear he looked a bit disappointed that no one else liked his name.

In a second Frankie's eyes went from regular goldfish white to swirling green.

'Pradeep!' I whispered – pointing at Frankie.

'Oh no,' said Pradeep. 'His zombie goldfish sense must be telling him something evil is going on.'

At that moment, the last knight in the tournament stepped forward. He was all in black. Black armour, black helmet and black shield. He was tall and broad and stood perfectly still, waiting to be introduced.

'It seems we haveth a latecomer to the tournament . . .' Motley Fool began. He frowned at his list of knights. 'But I hast not a name for this noble knight.'

Mark suddenly stood up and shouted out, 'I was talking to him earlier and he said his name was . . . ummmm . . . errr . . . Knight.'

'Simply, "Knight"?' Motley Fool asked.

'Nnno, *Nnnnight!*' Sanj stood up and shouted. 'Becnnnause he is blannnck as nnnnight.'

'I am sorry, noble sir, what language doeth thou speaketh?' Motley Fool asked.

Mark interrupted, 'Ummm. It's "Night", like black as the night. So he's like . . . a Night Knight! Yeah, cool.'

'Welcome, noble Night Knight!' Motley Fool jingled, and the crowd clapped again.

The contest had begun and Frankie seemed to have calmed down, although he kept sticking his head out of the flagon and looking around suspiciously.

'It must have been Mark and Sanj that set off Frankie's zombie senses,' I said to Pradeep, who nodded, not taking his eyes off the archers. The

Knight of the Rose had landed his first arrow within the smallest circle. Then the Knight of the Crown fired, and his shot was also close to the centre of the target.

'That was nearly a bullseye!' One of the Lords shouted.

'Hey, why is the centre of a target called a bullseye?' I asked.

'In archery it isn't, actually,' said Pradeep. 'If you hit the central yellow ring it's called "hitting the gold".'

The third knight was about to shoot. The Knight-Mare aimed his arrow carefully, then drew back his bow and fired. The arrow hit the target square in the centre.

'Good "hitting the gold"!' I shouted. The crowd looked up at me with a joint expression that read, 'WHAT?'

'They obviously don't appreciate real archery,' Pradeep said and sighed.

The Night Knight was the final archer to

compete. I caught sight of Sanj fiddling with his wizard's wand, pointing it towards the knight.

'Do you think Sanj actually believes he has magical powers?' I joked, pointing at him.

Just then the Night Knight pulled back his bow in one strong but jerky motion. He paused for a second to shift his aim . . . then fired. The arrow hurtled through the air and drove straight into the shaft of the Knight-Mare's arrow, splitting it clean in two. The crowd

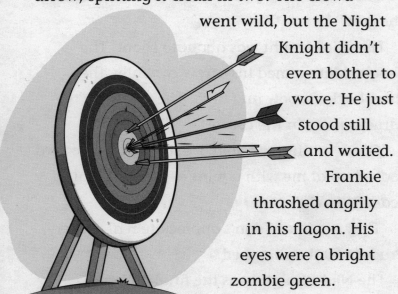

went wild, but the Night Knight didn't even bother to wave. He just stood still and waited. Frankie thrashed angrily in his flagon. His eyes were a bright zombie green.

Pradeep tapped me on the shoulder. He was pointing at Mark who was standing up and holding his hat in a way that looked like he was hiding something. Mark looked over at Sanj and nodded. Sanj smiled.

'What are they up to?' I said to Pradeep.

CHAPTER 5

A KNIGHT THAT'S NOT ALL RIGHT

'What a triumphant victory for the noble Night Knight!' Motley Fool shouted. 'Never before hath I seen such shooting.' He shook his jingly stick and the applause died down. 'We haveth a victor of the first competition, but who shall be crowneth the champion of all?'

With that the Night Knight strode jerkily past the other knights, out of the arena and into the crowd. He headed around the walls towards the back of the castle.

'The knights will now partake in some refreshment,' Motley Fool announced. 'Your morning activities shall commence forthwith.'

Frankie's eyes had gone back to a normal colour but he still looked edgy.

'Maybe we should get Frankie something to eat to calm him down?' I suggested.

We climbed down and followed a trail of green slime that was dripping from the side of the castle walls, pulling bits off for Frankie to chew on. Zombie goldfish only eat green food, the mouldier and slimier the better, but Frankie also has a thing for green sweets. We were so busy collecting slime that we didn't even notice that we had walked up to the Night Knight until we were standing right next to him.

'Er, hello, Sir Night Knight,' I said in surprise. Frankie's eyes flashed green, so I quickly pushed him into the flagon and covered the top with my hand.

The Night Knight didn't even look at us.

'Um, could we just get to that bit of green wall behind you please?' Pradeep added as we tried to squeeze past. 'We're collecting slime for . . . er, a *project* . . .'

Just as we started scraping off some really gooey bits, The Knight-Mare walked up and tapped the Night Knight on the shoulder.

The black knight didn't move.

'Um . . .' began the Knight-Mare. 'Sir Night Knight . . . I just wanted to say that I admired your shooting out there. Excellent aim. You deserved to win.'

The Night Knight just stood there – his helmet visor covering his face. Then he shoved past the Knight-Mare and marched away.

The Knight-Mare's shoulders slumped and a little sigh came out of his visor. 'Oh . . . OK,' he mumbled.

Pradeep looked at me, then said, 'Excuse me, Sir Knight-Mare, your shooting was brilliant. In any other contest – you would totally have won.'

'And you definitely have the coolest name,' I added.

'Oh, thanks.' The knight lifted up his visor, and we could see that he wasn't a big scary bearded man like I'd imagined. He looked really young actually. Like a teenager.

'It's my first tournament,' he admitted. 'I was a squire until last week in medieval club. I thought the name would make me sound, you know, tough. More tough than my real name,' he added.

'What *is* your real name?' Pradeep asked.

'Sebastian,' the knight mumbled. 'Not exactly a name that strikes terror into the heart of your opponents, is it?'

'It probably depends how you say it,' I said. 'Sebaaaaastiiiiaaan!' I tried. 'SEB – AS – TI – AN.' I shook my head. 'Nope, you're right. It just doesn't work.'

'It doesn't matter anyway,' said Sebastian sadly. 'With the Night Knight on the scene there's no way I'll win.'

'Do you think there's something a little bit

weird about the Night Knight?' Pradeep asked Sebastian.

'He's not very friendly, that's for sure,' said Sebastian. 'Right, I have to go and practise for the boulder lifting. It's not my best event.'

'What is?' Pradeep asked.

'The jousting.' Sebastian smiled. 'I have the best horse ever for the joust. Guinevere. That's why I wanted to be a squire in the first place – to look after the horses. Then the people who ran medieval club found out I could shoot really well so they trained me up to be a knight.' He pulled a paper bag from a pocket under his chest plate. 'I got Guinevere some special sugar cubes in different colours as a treat. Look,' he opened the bag. 'Pink, yellow, orange, green . . .'

As soon as Sebastian said 'green', Frankie shoved my hand away from the top of the flagon and burst out, landing on Sebastian's armoured gauntlet.

'Arrrrggggggghhhhh!' the Knight-Mare

screamed, dropping the sugar cubes and Frankie
to the ground.

'Frankie!' I shouted at him.

'Please excuse our goldfish's manners,'
Pradeep said, scooping up Frankie and popping
him in the flagon again.

'He just really, *really* likes green food,' I
added, scrambling around on the floor for the
fallen cubes.

'I can see that,' Sebastian said. 'He dropped a green sugar cube into the flagon after Frankie.' A satisfied burp came from inside.

'Did your fish . . . Oh, no. You'll think I'm going crazy,' Sebastian started.

'Did he what?' I asked.

'Did he fire pebbles at one of the trumpets just before the archery tournament started?' Sebastian asked.

Pradeep and I looked embarrassed. 'Oh. Yeah, that was him,' I said.

'Thank goodness!' said Sebastian. 'I thought the nerves had got to me and I was seeing things! He's not bad.'

Frankie popped his head out of the flagon and glared at Sebastian.

'OK! He's very good.' Sebastian smiled. 'I've never seen a pet fish do that before. Actually I've never seen a pet fish do anything before but swim in circles.'

'Frankie's kind of special,' I said.

Just then I heard Mrs Richards behind us. 'Boys!' she called. 'You are going to be late for bread making. It's about to start!'

'We've got to go,' I said, popping the cork back into Frankie's flagon.

'See you at the next event, Sebastian,' Pradeep said. 'I mean, Sir Knight-Mare!'

Sebastian waved us off and headed towards the stables.

I shot Pradeep a look that said, 'Whatever is going on with the Night Knight must have something to do with Mark and Sanj. We can't waste our time making bread when there is investigating to do!'

'Wait until we get to the kitchens,' Pradeep's look replied. 'I think I have a plan.'

CHAPTER 6
SIR FRANKIE OF ORANGE

'Eacheth morsel of bread on the table of the King once started as a grain of wheat crush-ed herein,' Motley Fool explained.

'You said you might have a plan?' I whispered to Pradeep as we sat at a work bench, pounding at some wheat with some grinding stones.

'While everyone is busy, we get Frankie to hypnotize Motley Fool so he won't notice if we slip away,' Pradeep whispered back. 'No one will notice a couple of peasants running errands around the castle. We're already wearing the perfect disguise!'

We waited until Mrs Richards had stepped

out to take some kids to the castle loos.

'Now's our chance!' Pradeep said.

I opened the flagon. 'Are you ready, Frankie?'
He nodded.

I hung the flagon from a beam that was
directly in Motley Fool's eyeline. Frankie peeked
out and his eyes started to swirl in glowing,
zombie green circles. The fool started talking
more and more slowly. 'The process of *swishy
fishy* kneading the *swishy fishy* dough into loaves
swishy fishy is a long and . . .'

'It's working,' Pradeep whispered. 'Now make
him fall asleep, Frankie.'

Everyone else was busy kneading their bread
dough, so not many kids even noticed when
Motley Fool started napping instead of speaking.

Pradeep and I got up, unhooked Frankie's
flagon and tiptoed out of the kitchen. Just as
we stepped out of the door we saw a familiar
little kitten disappear around the corner of the
corridor ahead. Frankie thrashed in his flagon.

'Fang!' Pradeep and I said at the same time.

'I should have known that Mark's evil vampire kitten would be involved,' I said. 'This definitely means Mark and Sanj are up to something evil.'

'Maybe she'll lead us to their secret medieval lair?' Pradeep said.

As we followed Fang around the corner, we could hear Mrs Richards's voice coming from the top of the staircase ahead. 'The historically accurate privies are part of the castle exhibition. You may look at them but *DO NOT USE THEM!*' she boomed. '*No.* Use the modern toilets in the block next door like everyone else. Hurry up. Have you washed your hands? Well go back and wash them. We are using these hands to make bread, aren't we? WASH THEM. NOW.'

'Ohhh, a kitten!' a girl's voice squealed.

Fang must have run past her and into the toilets!

'In medieval times, cats were kept not as pets, but as pest-control, to keep the mice in the castle at bay,' Mrs Richards said. 'They have really thought of everything.'

We skidded to a halt at the top of the stairs.

'Now everyone's hands are clean, let's go back down to the kitchens,' said the teacher.

'She'll see us,' I said, looking around for a hiding place. 'Quick . . . let's hide on that ledge.'

I put down Frankie's flagon and pushed open an old metal and glass window that pivoted

around a bar in the middle. I squeezed out first
and then Pradeep scrambled out on to the first-
floor ledge after me. We shuffled along so that
we were standing on either side of the window
out of sight.

Pradeep looked down, then over at me with
wide eyes. 'We are balanced on a ledge outside
a castle over a moat, hiding from a teacher
and chasing an evil kitten,' he whispered. 'This
is exactly the kind of thing I didn't want to be
doing today.'

We heard footsteps as Mrs Richards and the
kids walked past.

'Miss,' said a girl's voice. 'Someone's left their
drink behind.'

I looked at Pradeep with a look that said, 'She
doesn't mean Frankie's flagon, does she? You
picked that up, right?'

Pradeep shook his head.

'It must belong to someone at the castle,' said
Mrs Richards. 'Hang it up there in the historical

privies and someone will find it.'

We waited for their footsteps to fade away
and had just started shuffling back towards
the window when we saw two small furry paws
pushing the window closed and heard the sound
of a latch snapping into place.

'Nooooo!' we both cried.

CHAPTER 7
QUEEN FANG

'I can't believe that evil kitten just locked us outside!' I huffed. Suddenly we heard the sound of Fang screeching and the thwacking of fins against stone.

'I think Fang and Frankie have found each other!' said Pradeep. 'We've got to get in there!'

'Look, there's another open window over there.' I pointed along the ledge.

Carefully we shuffled along until we reached the opening. Pradeep sniffed the air. 'Pine-scented bleach . . . this must be the toilet window!'

Inside we could still hear the sounds of miaows and fins flapping.

'Frankie's been out of his flagon for ages now!' I said. 'He must need water. Why doesn't he just jump into one of the toilets?'

Pradeep had one of those moments where you could tell he was going through all the files in his head, flipping past all the unlikely explanations until he came to the only reasonable answer. He does this a lot faster than me because I tend to get distracted by things that probably wouldn't *ever* happen but would be funny if they did.

His face switched to his 'Got it!' look. 'Because these are drop toilets,' he replied. 'They must be the historically accurate ones that Mrs Richards was talking about. No running water, just a drop to the moat below.'

We scrambled in through the window. Frankie

and Fang were locked in combat. Frankie was looking tired, while Fang seemed ready for another pounce. I quickly grabbed the flagon from where it had been left and flung it at Fang. It only startled her for a second, but that was all Frankie needed.

'Head for the toilet!' Pradeep shouted to Frankie. 'We'll find you in the moat later!'

Frankie looked over at us.

'Go, Frankie,' I shouted.

Frankie heaved himself over the edge of the stone toilet and tumbled down through the hole. Fang sprang after him, but when she realized there was nothing but a drop to the moat below she soon changed her mind.

There was a splash as Frankie hit the water and disappeared underneath.

CHAPTER 8
A BANQUET FIT FOR A FISH

Fang spat angrily from her perch on the top of the stone toilet. 'Hiiiiiiiissssssss!'

'What on earth is this racket?' Mrs Richard's voice boomed around the historically accurate privies.

Fang jumped in terror and shot straight past the teacher and down the stairs, screeching as she ran.

'Just what are you two doing?' Mrs Richards tutted at us. 'Even though Motley Fool fell asleep, that's no excuse to go roaming the halls.'

'We were . . . ummm . . .' Pradeep started.

'We were rescuing the cat,' I lied with my

fingers crossed behind my back. 'We heard miaowing and . . . er . . .'

'Came in here to find the cat in distress,' Pradeep continued. Which was technically true.

'And then she nearly fell through the toilet hole but didn't,' I added. Which was also true.

'Oh, really?' Mrs Richards looked at us as if she was trying to decide if we were telling the truth. 'I suppose that is very chivalrous of you.'

'Huh?' I said.

'Chivalry is one of the principles of knighthood,' Pradeep said. 'It means gallant and well-mannered.'

'Yeah, I guess we were being that,' I

said, crossing my fingers again.

'Right, well, it's lunchtime now,' said the teacher, 'so come with me to the great hall. Motley Fool has already taken the rest of the class in.'

'Umm, I think I dropped something down the historically accurate toilet while we were . . . um . . . saving the cat,' I said.

'If you dropped something in the moat then it's gone, sorry.' Mrs Roberts had a stern look on her face. I knew I couldn't push it. Frankie would have to wait.

I picked up the flagon from the floor where I had thrown it very *unchivalrously* at Fang, and followed Mrs Richards down the stairs and through the castle.

Inside the great hall, all the peasants were already sitting down at simple tables along the walls. The merchants, soldiers and traders were sitting in comfy chairs at long tables in the middle of the room, and the Lords and Ladies and special guests were all at the top tables on a raised platform at the front.

The trumpeters started playing again and everyone stood up as the four competing knights took their places at the centre of the top table. All of the knights removed their helmets as they sat down, except for the Night Knight.

I could see Motley Fool trying to talk to him, but the Night Knight was totally blanking him. Pradeep nudged me and pointed at Sanj who was once again fiddling with his wand.

Motley Fool tried again. This time the Night Knight shook his head, and Motley Fool bowed and waved away the plate of bread and soup that a servant was about to put down.

The other knights were already tucking in, and baskets of bread and platters of fruit and meat were being placed on their tables as well.

I looked at the slop in the wooden bowl in front of me. 'Frankie would love this,' I said,

stirring my green gruel. 'I hope he's OK.'

'Just because we haven't been able to go and look for Frankie doesn't mean he won't be able to find us,' Pradeep said. 'I'm sure he'll find a way.'

I looked over at the top tables to see the goblets being filled by people pretending to be servants. Sebastian held out his cup.

As a servant poured his water,

I could have sworn I saw a fleck of orange tumble out of the jug and into the Knight-Mare's goblet.

CHAPTER 9

A GOBLET OF GOLDFISH

'I think I just saw Frankie,' I whispered to Pradeep.

Sebastian quickly put his hand over the cup and looked around, searching the crowd until he spotted Pradeep and me. His look said, quite clearly, 'Excuse me but I believe your fish is in my goblet?'

We gave him the thumbs-up and my look said, 'Hang on, we'll come and get him.'

At that moment Motley Fool raised his glass and motioned for everyone else to do the same.

'A toast,' he said. 'To all the noble Ladies and Gentlemen who hast provided us this feast.'

The Knight of the Crown, the
Knight of the Rose and Sebastian
all raised their glasses. The Night
Knight didn't move.

'Will you not toast our hosts,
noble sir?' Motley Fool asked him, but again, the
Night Knight was still.

'That's a huge insult,' Pradeep whispered.
'And really unchivalrous too. No real knight
would do that.'

'They are all *pretend* knights, Pradeep,' I said.
'Sebastian is a horse trainer at a medieval club,
the Crown guy is probably a dentist, and the
Rose guy probably works in a garden centre. This
is *all* pretend.'

'Chivalry is *real*,' Pradeep muttered.

Just then Mark grabbed Sanj's wand and the
Night Knight jerked his goblet upwards.

Motley Fool smiled. 'To our noble hosts!'

Everyone repeated what he'd said, then
sipped their drinks. Well, everyone but the Night

Knight, who lifted his goblet up to his visor and then poured the contents all down his front. Sanj grabbed the wand back off Mark and they started bickering in whispers.

For a second I thought I saw a spark and a twitch from the Night Knight, before a servant dabbed at the spill with a cloth.

'That was strange,' I whispered to Pradeep.

'Strange and suspicious,' he said.

'Strange suspicious and *mostly evil*,' I added. 'We've got to get a closer look at the Night Knight.'

'And that magic wand,' Pradeep said.

'We've got a bigger problem right now though,' I said, looking at Sebastian, who looked exactly like he had a mouthful of unhappy goldfish!

Pradeep smiled. 'Of course! The toast. It would have been unchivalrous not to drink, even if you have a zombie goldfish in your cup. That's the sign of a true knight.'

'I think that true knight needs our help,' I said. 'Come on!'

We raced up to the top table and held Pradeep's hat in front of Sebastian's face just as he 'belched' the water and fish into the hat.

I quickly covered the contents with my cloak.

'Thank you, young peasant.' Sebastian gave us a relieved look. 'I suddenly felt very unwell.'

Then he whispered, 'I didn't think when I sipped from the cup the fish would jump into my mouth!'

'No worries . . . um . . . I mean . . . it is our duty to help you, Sir Knight . . . Person.' I bowed and then whispered, 'Sorry, he does that. I think he just wanted to get back to us.'

Pradeep added, 'Thanks for not giving Frankie away. Good luck with the boulder lift!'

We backed away with the hat still covered until we found Mrs Richards. 'Miss, is it OK if we go and wash this out?' I asked.

'Of course!' she cried, trying not to go anywhere near the hat. 'Then come and join us in the courtyard for the next tournament challenge.'

Once we were outside we uncovered the hat.

'Frankie, are you OK?' I asked.

He nodded.

'Do you know what's up with the Night Knight?' added Pradeep. 'Is he part of an evil plan?'

Frankie nodded again, then started stiffly marching through the water in the hat.

'The Night Knight is a soldier?' Pradeep guessed.

Frankie shook his head. He put his arms out and walked stiffly without marching.

'He's a mummy?' I said.

Both Frankie and Pradeep gave me a look that said, 'Really, that's your guess?'

Frankie shook his head. Then he started blowing water bubbles to spell 'Beep, beep, beep!'

'The Night Knight is a car?' I asked.

Frankie hung his head.

'Oh, no!' Pradeep shouted. Then he said in a lower voice, 'I think Frankie's saying . . . he *thinks* Night Knight is a robot!'

CHAPTER 10

THE NOT SO SECRET OF THE NIGHT KNIGHT

Frankie nodded and his eyes flashed green.

'The Night Knight is a robot!' I cried. 'That explains the sparks we saw.'

'And the not eating and the jerky movements,' Pradeep added.

'And his amazing archery shooting,' I said. 'Are you sure, Frankie?'

Frankie shrugged.

'Then we've got to find out,' Pradeep said.

We poured Frankie from Pradeep's hat back into the flagon just as our class approached.

'Ah, I see you've cleaned your hat then,' said

Mrs Richards to Pradeep. 'Now come along, boys, or you'll be late for the boulder-lift challenge.'

We made our way back to the tournament area in the courtyard, where there was a large boulder in the centre of the grassy competitors' arena.

The knights stood around it, and bowed as the Lords and Ladies slowly took their seats on the platform. This time, each knight had his horse tethered close by – ready for the final event – the joust. The horses all had the emblems of their knights on their saddles, except for the large black horse with a black saddle and head cover. Sebastian was standing near the edge of the arena by a white mare. He patted her nose and gave her a sugar lump from his palm. That must be Guinevere.

Motley Fool jingled his stick. 'Lords and Ladies, shall we maketh ready for the second challenge of the tournament?' He paused. 'The test of strength?'

The crowd cheered. We could see Sanj and Mark sitting at opposite ends of the stands with their schools. Mark had his hat positioned as before – as if he was hiding something, while Sanj had his wand pointed at the Night Knight.

'I'll go and check out what Mark's up to,' I whispered to Pradeep, handing him the flagon with Frankie inside. 'You keep an eye on Sanj and see if you can get Frankie closer to the Night Knight.'

The Knight of the Crown stepped up to the boulder. He bent down and with both hands managed to lift it off the ground and up to his knees before he dropped it again.

Everyone applauded.

By the time the Knight of the Rose had taken his place, I had made my way underneath the stands and was hiding just below Mark's row of seats. I couldn't see Fang anywhere, but I knew she must be close by.

Through the gap between the seats, I saw the Knight of the Rose lift the boulder up as high as his waist. Then he started shaking and let it go. Mark put his hat down on the floor by his feet while he clapped. 'Hah! Loser,' he cackled. 'You are going down like the rest of them.'

In total stealth mode, I silently reached up and tilted back the edge of Mark's hat. Hidden inside was a small digital camera! Mark was videoing the challenges. But why? We were told not to bring any phones or cameras today. I ducked back down and snuck away while Sebastian was taking his place.

'The Night-Mare!' Motley Fool announced as I got back to Pradeep's side.

Sebastian picked up the stone and lifted it to his waist. He lifted it a little higher, then a little more. I noticed Sanj shoot Mark a look, then Mark reached in his pocket and pulled out a slingshot and a water balloon.

'Look!' shouted Sanj suddenly. 'A crow . . . wearing a hat!' When everyone turned to see where he was pointing, Mark fired the water balloon at Guinevere.

The horse whinnied and reared up. Sebastian immediately turned to her and dropped the boulder. 'Argggggghhhhh!' he screamed, hopping on one foot! 'My toe!'

Pradeep and I ran up to the fence around the arena.

'Are you OK?' I called to Sebastian.

'I think I've broken my toe,' the knight shouted back. 'Is Guinevere all right? I heard her whinny like she was hurt.'

'I think she was just startled by something. We'll check on her,' Pradeep cried.

'I know what startled Guinevere,' I whispered to Pradeep. 'It was Mark! He fired a water balloon at her. He's also secretly filming the tournament.'

While Sebastian was carried off to the medical tent, Pradeep and I rushed over to where Guinevere was tethered at the side of the arena to try and calm her down.

'There, girl,' I said, trying to pat her side through the fence, but she wouldn't stop stomping and I couldn't get close.

Frankie popped up out of the flagon of water in Pradeep's hands. He jumped over the fence and on to Guinevere's nose, his eyes glowing a bright zombie green. In a moment she was whinnying quietly, with one eye staring at the fence and her other staring up Pradeep's left

nostril. I quickly scooped Frankie back into the flagon before anyone could see him.

'Thanks, Frankie,' I whispered.

'So,' said Pradeep. 'Mark and Sanj must really want the Night Knight – who may or may not be an evil robot – to win this competition. And they need evidence of this on video. The question is, why?'

'I don't know,' I replied. 'But now we have a zombified horse to deal with too! What else could possibly go wrong?'

CHAPTER 11

EXIT STAGE LEFT, PURR-SUING KITTEN

As the word 'wrong' left my mouth, Fang shot across the courtyard, scrambled over a wall near the stands and headed for the stairs to one of the castle's turrets.

'You have *got* to stop saying things like that!' Pradeep grumbled.

'Never mind,' I whispered back. 'Something tells me if we follow Fang we'll find out more about the Night Knight.'

'There's nothing we can do while Guinevere is hypnotized and Sebastian is being treated in the medical tent,' Pradeep replied. 'Let's go.'

As we took a shortcut under the stands, I saw that Mark had put his slingshot and water balloons down by his feet. I reached up and took them. At least I could make sure that he couldn't shoot at any of the horses again.

I shoved them down the back of my tights and ran to catch up with Pradeep. There is a basic design flaw in peasant costumes with them not having pockets. Peasants must have had stuff to carry, right? I just don't believe they just carried everything in their tights.

As we got to the doorway at the bottom of the turret steps, Pradeep held a finger to his lips to mean 'Shhhhh'. Then he made a sign for 'cat' with his hands and pointed up the stairs.

I nodded and we began to climb.

When we got to the top we found ourselves in the doorway of a circular room. It had tall narrow windows with no glass in them and a couple of wooden chairs and a table in the middle. Frankie's eyes shone a bright green, giving the room a creepy glow.

'Mark and Sanj must have been using this as their evil medieval lair,' Pradeep whispered.

Their stuff was on the table and on the floor. Backpacks, computer stuff, wires, tools, and blueprints for something . . . we both stepped forward to take a closer look.

BOOM! The door to the room slammed shut behind us and we heard an evil purr and the sound of a key turning in the lock.

'Fang!' we both cried. Pradeep ran to the door and jiggled the handle but it was no good. We were trapped.

By now Frankie had wriggled out of his flagon and was flinging himself at the crack under the door, trying to squeeze himself through.

'It's no good, Frankie, you're too big,' I said. 'That evil kitten tricked us.'

'*Again*,' added Pradeep gloomily. He held out the flagon for Frankie to jump back in.

Suddenly a small piece of parchment was pushed under the door. Pradeep picked it up and we started to read.

As you'll have guessed by now the kitten has tricked you and you are our prisoners in the tower. (Insert evil laugh here.) For this part of the plan to have been enacted you must have:

* Realized that the Night Knight is an incredibly intricately designed, hyper-strong and accurate robot warrior.
* Suspected that we are the creators and

operators of this amazing, potentially ground-breaking creation in the world of Evil Science, which we like to think of as the Mona Lisa of robotics

Then the writing changed to more of a Mark-like scrawl . . .

* Or brought the moron fish with you, which would totally have wrecked things so you all had to be taken out of the picture.

Regardless, you are now trapped, with no means of escape until the end of the day, when the parents come to see the final joust and take their kids home afterwards. I suppose then someone might go looking for you up there.

Oh, yes and to deter you from shouting for help, Fang will now switch on a loud recording of

crows 'cawwwwing' that will mask any screams or shouts from the tower.

We heard a click of a button from outside the door and then some speakers on the walls by the tower windows stared blaring out loud crow sounds.

See, we really have thought of everything. (Insert second evil laugh here.) Enjoy your stay in the tower . . .

Then the writing changed again.

Yeah, morons. Have fun staring at these four walls while we are winning the whole tournament! Result!
Actually there is only one wall as it is a circular room. Just to be accurate.
Who cares about that? It was just meant to sound scary, dude.

It doesn't take any more time to be both scary and accurate.

Then there are just scribbles that look like they were fighting over the pen.

Pradeep scrunched up the piece of paper and threw it at the floor. Then he picked it up again and put it on the table. It hurts Pradeep to litter, even in anger.

'I'm not even going to say that I can't believe that we fell for the old "follow-the-kitten-into-the-isolated-turret trick", because I totally *can* believe we fell for it,' Pradeep said.

I went to the window to see what was happening in the courtyard below.

I could see Sebastian outside the medical tent having his foot bandaged. Guinevere still looked

pretty zombified and the Night Knight was in the centre of the arena standing by the boulder.

Pradeep started looking through Sanj and Mark's stuff.

'Hey, look at this!' he called over the sound of crows. 'I think I found something.'

CHAPTER 12
BLUEPRINT FOR EVIL

Pradeep held up some blueprints of a robot knight. And there was a blueprint for a magic

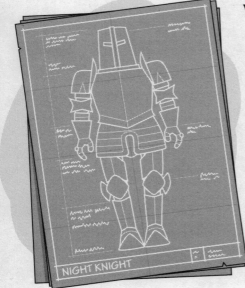

wand-shaped remote control too. Then he held up a flyer advertising a contest from *Evil Scientist Magazine* for 'Most Evil Robot' and read it out:

'The winner of the best design will gain automatic

NIGHT KNIGHT

membership to the Society of Evil Robot Makers and the chance to see their design mass-produced in our evil robot factory.' There was some small print too. Pradeep squinted and read on. '. . . All robots must be in good working order, with accompanying plans and all powers and abilities documented by video image.'

'So the Night Knight *is* an evil robot!' I gasped. 'And that's why Mark has been filming the tournament! To document its powers!'

'I guess that's why they entered him in the contest,' Pradeep added. 'When else could you have a robot openly firing arrows, lifting boulders or riding horses? This medieval reconstruction day is the perfect cover.'

I looked out the window again and held up Frankie in his flagon so he could see too. The Night Knight was starting to lift the boulder. He already had it at his waist. 'He'll beat Sebastian easily,' I said. 'Then it will all be over . . . they'll win the *Evil Scientist* competition and there's nothing we can do to stop them.'

We both thought about what Mark and Sanj would be like with an army of evil Night Knights at their command. It was not a good thought.

I went to slump down on the floor and then remembered the slingshot and water balloons in my tights. Now, you might be thinking, 'How could you forget there is a slingshot and two water balloons in your tights?' but I'd had a lot to think about in the last few minutes. I pulled them out and showed them to Pradeep. 'Maybe we can't stop the Night Knight, but we might be able to slow him down . . .'

I loaded up the first balloon and took aim.

Pradeep scanned the blueprints, looking for a weak spot where the water could get through.

'Shoot for the Night Knight's visor or hands,' he said. 'There are gaps to allow movement and the water might get through.'

I aimed for the visor first. The water balloon flew from the slingshot and just clipped the head of the knight. I thought I saw a couple of sparks but it didn't make the robot drop the boulder. He had it at chest height now and was still lifting. I aimed for its hand next. I only had one balloon left, so I had to make it count. This time I got a direct hit! The Night Knight's left hand started to shake and then went still.

Mark and Sanj started jumping up and down, and Sanj bashed the wand against his own hand.

The Night Knight had stopped.

'We did it!' I shouted and went to high-fin Frankie, but he nodded towards the Night Knight and shook his head. I couldn't believe it! The Night Knight had moved the boulder to his right hand and was now lifting it over his head.

The crowd gasped and oooohed.

Finally he stepped back and let the boulder thud to the floor!

'I thinketh we have a clear victor!' Motley Fool's voice echoed up over the cawing of crows from the tower. 'We shall now taketh a short break to prepareth the noble steeds and ready ourselves for the final challenge – the joust!'

He directed his next speech to the crowd of people just arriving at the drawbridge gate.

'Welcome, kin of the castle young folk. Thou shalt be escorted to the viewing stands on the castle side of the jousting area. You may findeth your child's class and accompany them should you wisheth.'

'I know your mum couldn't come, but my mum will be here any minute with Sami,' Pradeep said. 'We've got to get down there.'

'And we have to see if Sebastian can still joust!' I added. 'Someone has to stop the Night Knight and Mark and Sanj!'

Pradeep was looking at the windows and the door and pacing out how many steps were between them. Then he started doing some maths on a sheet of paper that Sanj had marked 'Evil To Do List'.

'I think I may have figured out a way to get Frankie to the other side of the door.' Pradeep peered through the keyhole. 'It looks like Fang left the key in the lock.'

'But Frankie's too big to fit under the door?' I said.

'But he's not too big to go through the window – and neither is the slingshot,' Pradeep answered.

CHAPTER 13
FOILED BY A FLYING FISH

Pradeep drew a picture to explain his plan.
We were going to shoot Frankie out of the slit
window with the slingshot and fire him over
the top of the turret. Then he would parachute
down, steering himself through the window
on the stairs. Then
all Frankie had
to do was pull
the key out of
the lock with his
mouth and push
it through the gap
under the door so we

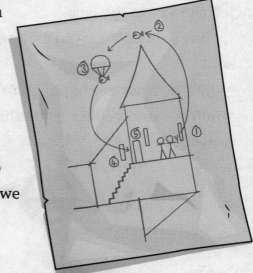

could unlock ourselves and be free.

Frankie peered up out of the flagon and nodded.

'We don't exactly have a goldfish parachute lying around though,' I said.

'Yes we do.' Pradeep smiled and took a neatly folded handkerchief out from his pocket. 'See, all we have to do is attach—'

'Hang on,' I interrupted Pradeep. 'You have pockets in your peasant costume?'

'Oh, yeah, Mum sewed them in,' Pradeep answered. 'I know it's not historically accurate but who wants to go around without pockets?'

I shrugged.

'All we need to do is attach some thread to the ends to make it a parachute. It will definitely support Frankie's weight,' Pradeep explained.

'We just need some thread,' I said and started to pull out the stitching from around the edge of my tunic. 'This should do.'

We tied the edges of the handkerchief to the

thread and then gave the knotted ends to Frankie to clamp down on with his jaw. Then we gently scooped him up and put him in the cradle of the slingshot.

'Are you ready, Frankie?' I asked.

'Just steer your parachute towards the stairway window and you'll be fine,' Pradeep said.

I leaned both arms out the window and aimed directly upward.

'A little bit to the right, now up a bit, a bit more, there . . .' Pradeep said. 'Now fire!'

'Be careful, Frankie!' I whispered. I pulled back on the slingshot and sent Frankie soaring.

We ran to the opposite window to see if we could see Frankie's parachute hanky.

Sure enough, a few seconds later a white parachute with a delicately embroidered 'PK' on one corner sailed past the window carrying one very wind-blown-looking goldfish.

Frankie disappeared from view, but we heard the gentle flutter of a handkerchief and the

thwap of a
goldfish
hitting
the floor
as Frankie
landed on
the other side
of the door.

In a second
we heard the
key clunk down to the
floor. Frankie nudged it under
the door with his tail, and I quickly
opened the lock and scooped Frankie into his
water-filled flagon.

'Well done, Frankie!' I cried.

He winked at me as if to say, 'Hey, I'm a
professional. I do this kind of thing all the time!'

I grabbed the blueprints and shoved them
down my tights before we raced down the stairs.

*

Instead of going into the courtyard at the bottom of the stairs, we crept along the main hall, past all the old suits of armour and shields on display. The hall led to an exit by the stables, which is where we hoped we'd find Sebastian.

We were right.

'There you are' he said, hobbling over. 'I've been looking for you. My big toe is sprained so I can't compete . . . but you're right, there is something strange about the Night Knight. I think he's cheating, which is definitely not in the knights' code of conduct. We've got to prove he's not playing by the rules, but I don't know how.'

'Well, we think the Night Knight is actually an evil robot,' I said.

'A what?' Sebastian shook his head.

'Well, more like a giant remote-controlled toy,' Pradeep corrected me.

'Our evil big brothers made him to win some kind of contest,' I added. 'If they win there will be lots more Night Knight robots . . . all under Mark and Sanj's control.'

'If the Night Knight is a robot then we have to report it. It's the right thing to do,' Sebastian said. He called over Motley Fool, who was walking past with some jousting poles.

'Excuse me, Mr Fool,' Sebastian said. 'I need to report that the Night Knight is competing under false pretences.'

'What say you, sir?' Motley Fool answered. 'That is a serious allegation thou hast made.'

'Yes, but it's true. On my honour, sir, I believe the Night Knight to be a robot.'

Motley Fool looked at Sebastian and then broke into a full belly laugh. 'Why, sir, thou hast made a goodly jest! Now we'll have no more interruptions. I must make haste to start the jousting.'

He handed Sebastian one of the jousting poles.

'Robot? Next thing he'll tell me it's an evil robot!' the fool mumbled to himself as he walked away.

'I knew they wouldn't believe us without proof,' I said. 'But we *might* be able to get some.'

Pradeep looked at me and then at the jousting pole that Sebastian was holding. 'It's a pretty big MIGHT though,' he said.

'Whatever it is, I shall help. Oh, and I think there's something up with Guinevere too. She seems a little dazed and confused,' Sebastian said.

Frankie peeked out of the flagon guiltily.

'Err . . . well, we wanted to help calm her down. So Frankie kind of hypnotized her,' I said.

'So your goldfish is a horse whisperer now?' Sebastian asked.

'More a horse zombifier,' Pradeep replied. 'But don't worry, there are no lasting side effects. My little sister has been zombified by Frankie dozens of times.'

With that we heard a distant cry of 'SWISHY FISHY! SWISHY FISHY!' and Sami, Pradeep's three-year-old little sister, came scampering across the stone floor from the other end of the hall, dressed as a medieval princess complete with pointy hat and veil.

CHAPTER 14

THE PRINCESS AND HER GOLDFISH

Sami ran straight up to us and grabbed Frankie in the flagon to give him a big hug.

'Hi, Sami,' Pradeep said. 'Is Mum with you?'

'Mummy runs slow,' Sami said, and then she stopped and stared up at Sebastian in his full knight's armour. She held out her hand and knocked on his leg. 'Is knight real?' she asked.

'Hello, little princess,' Sebastian said and smiled. 'I am most certainly real, and I am at your service.' He did one of those bows where you wave your hand in front of your face in a really elegant knight way. If I did that I would look like I was swatting medieval flies.

Sami giggled and turned red. Then she curtsied. 'Mr Knight,' she said.

'This is my little sister Sami,' Pradeep said. 'Sami, this is Sebastian.' She thought for a second and pulled a face. 'Not knight name.' She shook her head.

'I know!' Sebastian smiled at Sami. 'So tell me your plan,' he said to us.

'If you can't do the joust then maybe Tom or I could do it in your place? We could pretend to be the Knight-Mare,' said Pradeep.

'Can either of you ride a horse?' asked Sebastian. 'Or handle a jousting pole? Or fit in my suit of armour?'

We both shook our heads. Maybe the plan wouldn't work after all.

Pradeep's mum came running up to where we were standing. 'Sami,' she said breathlessly. 'I've been calling to you since you ran across the drawbridge.'

'Whoopsie,' Sami said, and then turned to Sebastian. 'Look – real knight.'

Mrs Kumar held out her hand to shake Sebastian's, but he held it and kissed it lightly. 'I'm Sebastian, madam. A pleasure to meet you. You have a delightful daughter.'

'Oh, how lovely.' Mrs Kumar blushed as she spoke. Then she turned to Pradeep, gasped, and immediately grabbed a wet wipe out of her handbag to clean the mud off his tunic. 'I can't let you walk around the castle like this!' she tutted.

'Mum!' Pradeep mumbled. 'It's OK. All the other peasants are muddy.'

'Are they my peasants?' she answered. 'No.'

Sami tugged on Mrs Kumar's skirt. 'Me stay

with Pradeep?' She gave her mum the big soppy-eyes look. 'Please?'

'All right,' Mrs Kumar said and patted Sami on the head. 'I'll go and get us a drink. Pradeep, will you look after Sami? I'll be back in ten minutes. I hope to see you later as well, Mr Sebastian,' she called as she left for the drinks tent.

'We have to come up with another plan,' Pradeep whispered. 'But what?'

Suddenly Guinevere trotted up behind us and nudged Frankie's flagon with her nose. She still had the zombie stare and was very calm.

'I thought you were in the arena?' said Sebastian, stroking her nose. 'Did you just walk here all on your own? How did you know where to find us?'

Frankie winked at me from his flagon.

'Wait, I think I know how we can do this,' I said.

CHAPTER 15
HALF A KNIGHT-MARE

'We don't need to know how to ride a horse,' I told Sebastian as Sami stroked the white mare's mane. 'Frankie can control Guinevere so that she is safe and so are we.'

'Do you mean to say that Frankie is mind-controlling Guinevere right now?' Sebastian asked.

'Yeah, it's something he does a lot,' Pradeep admitted.

'But you can't compete out there without proper armour,' Sebastian said.

'We passed lots of suits of armour in the hall,' I replied.

'Yes, we can use one of those!' Pradeep added, running back into the hall. We left Guinevere in a stable pen and followed Pradeep inside. He stood next to one of the suits of armour, but he only came up as high as the waist.

'I'm sorry to say, I don't think they'll fit you,' Sebastian said with a smile.

Then I ran over and jumped on Pradeep's back and shoulders.

'Ugh!' muttered Pradeep.

'But it would fit both of us together,' I cried. I balanced Frankie's flagon on the hat on top of my head. 'And Frankie makes it a perfect fit.'

'Yes,' agreed Pradeep. 'That way Frankie can see to steer Guinevere and we can hold the jousting pole.'

'I don't know if this is safe,' Sebastian said. 'And your legs won't touch the floor – how will you walk?'

'We won't have to!' I said. 'We can get on to Guinevere in the stables, so no one will see us off the horse.'

'But the Night Knight is much, much stronger than you. Even with Frankie's help,' Sebastian persisted, 'how do you plan to stop him?'

Pradeep got that glow he gets when a really, *really* good plan starts to come together in his head. 'Well,' he said. 'We know that the Night Knight stops working if he gets too wet. So if we can get a jet of water to hit him in a vulnerable spot then we can stop him mid-joust.' He looked over at the pole Sebastian was holding.

My mind started catching up with Pradeep's.

'All we need to do is rig up the jousting pole like it's a really long water pistol,' I said.

'We make a chain of straws from the drinks stand and run them along the pole, right from the tip down to Frankie inside the flagon,' Pradeep said.

Frankie poked his head out of the top of the flagon and shot a jet of water at Sebastian.

'And you know he's a good shot!' I handed Sebastian the parachute handkerchief to dry his face.

Sebastian paused and looked at me and Pradeep, then at Frankie, and then at the suit of armour. 'Right, Tom, you go and get some straws from the drinks stand, I'll grab the suit of armour and bring it out to the stables, and let's get you two suited up and ready for a joust!' he said.

Sami jumped and clapped. 'Yaaay!'

'When you're ready I'll go and tell the judges that I have deputized my squire to take over for me for the event. It's within the rules for a squire to step in and you two are the closest thing to a squire that I have,' Sebastian added.

Pradeep and I rigged up the armour so the straw chain ran from the helmet, down the arm and all along the jousting pole. All Frankie had to do was shoot a spray of water through the straws, aiming at the Night Knight's visor.

Sebastian put the legs of the suit of armour on to Guinevere's back and then lifted up Pradeep so he could sit inside.

Next I was lifted up and the body of the suit of armour was attached. Finally, he balanced Frankie's flagon on my head by rolling

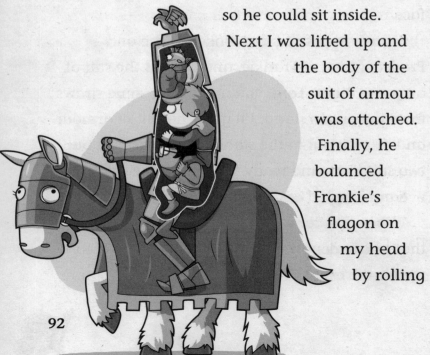

up both my and Pradeep's hats and using them to wedge the flagon into the helmet. I hadn't realized quite how dark it would be in a big metal suit of armour.

'I'll go and tell the judges now,' he said, once he was sure we were comfortable.

'You OK out there, Sami?' Pradeep mumbled.

'Yup!' Sami shouted.

I could hear the sounds of jousting going on out in the courtyard. Well, I assume it was jousting. It sounded like galloping horses and then the crashing, crumpling sound of metal hitting metal.

'Are you sure we'll be safe in this suit, Pradeep?' I asked.

'We only have to last long enough to spray the Night Knight with water,' he replied. 'We won't even get hit . . . hopefully.'

Footsteps approached and we felt the thud of a metal glove against the back plate of the armour. 'This is my trusted squire Pra . . . Tom,'

Sebastian's voice said. 'And this is Princess Sami.'

Sami giggled.

'Pra-tom?' a man's voice said, and I thought I heard a pencil scribbling on paper. 'That's an interesting name.'

'Mmmmm,' I agreed loudly from under the visor of the helmet.

'It's a shame you can't compete yourself, but the crowd will be glad that they are getting to see a final joust anyway,' the man said. 'The paperwork is in order. Good luck, Pra-tom. I think you'll need it,' he added under his breath.

Then we heard Sami squeal, 'Mummy look! Swishy fishy horsey!'

'Hello, Mrs Kumar,' Sebastian said. 'Perfect timing.' Then he spoke to Sami. 'Maybe you should go off with your mother now so that we can get . . . the knight here . . . ready for the joust.'

'OK,' Sami said. 'Bye bye swishy fishy horsey.'

'Have Pradeep and Tom gone off to see the

joust with their class then?' Mrs Kumar asked.

'Ahem,' coughed Sebastian. 'Er, they won't have the best view from where they're sitting, but they'll definitely be able to get a feel for the joust.'

'Right,' Mrs Kumar said. 'Come on then, princess.'

The next thing we knew, Guinevere had started walking. 'This is it!' I whispered.

'Mmph!' Pradeep whispered back. I think he was a bit squashed.

Then we heard Mrs Richards's voice. 'Excuse me, sir?' She must have been speaking to Sebastian. 'Have you seen two boys in peasant outfits over this way? They might have already gone to sit with their parents?'

Sebastian mumbled, 'Ummm . . . I think they've already taken their seats for the final joust. It's about to start.'

'Yes, that's probably where they are. Thank you,' she said.

'He managed to put both of them off without actually lying!' Pradeep mumbled. 'See, chivalry *is* real!'

'Respect,' I said. 'Sebastian,' I shouted out loud through the armour. 'Can you see Mark and Sanj anywhere? Sanj is dressed as a wizard and Mark is dressed as a Lord.'

Sebastian tapped on the armour. 'Yes, that must be them. They are on the far side of the courtyard speaking to the Night Knight. He's already on his horse.' He handed me the lance and fiddled with the straws to make sure they were all connected. 'OK, the Knights of the Rose

and the Crown are on their final pass. You guys are up next. Are you sure you want to do this?'

'We can't let the Night Knight win,' Pradeep said. 'It's just not chivalrous.'

'And we can't let Mark and Sanj enter the *Evil Scientist* competition. I don't even want to think about what our evil big brothers would do with an army of Night Knights,' I added.

Sebastian adjusted the lance so it was wedged under the arm of the suit of armour, secured the reins around my other gauntlet, and fed the end of the straw to Frankie in the helmet.

'When we get close enough, fire away, Frankie!' Pradeep mumbled. 'Tom, just hold on.'

'Check!' I said as Sebastian led Guinevere to the starting point for the joust. Then I heard a final clatter of horses' hoofs and a sound that sounded a lot like a knight breaking.

CHAPTER 16

SIR PRA-TOM THE CHIVALROUS

The trumpets sounded again and Motley Fool's voice boomed across the courtyard. 'Lords, Ladies and visiting guests of Castlerock Castle. Please be upstanding for the final joust of the day!'

The crowd clapped and cheered.

'Let us welcome . . . the Night Knight!' he shouted. We heard the stomping of hoofs and more cheering.

'And . . .' He paused. 'The noble squire of the Night-Mare . . . Pra-tom!'

The crowd cheered for us too.

'Now the dangerous and deadly tournament of the joust doth begin!'

'I think I might have changed my mind,' Pradeep said – just as Guinevere began her gallop.

We bounced along on the horse's back. I could hear the hoofs of the Night Knight's horse approaching and just as I thought we'd be trampled, I felt a dribble of water from the flagon as Frankie spat water through the straws on the lance.

But something was wrong. The Night Knight was still charging. His lance batted against ours at full gallop. I felt the full force and fell backwards. If the saddle hadn't had a back edge, I think we would have been pushed right off Guinevere's back!

'Frankie? Pradeep? Are you OK?' I mumbled as Guinevere galloped down the rest of the track.

'Why can't we ever just have a normal day out?' mumbled Pradeep, while Frankie splashed water on to my head to show he was all right.

When we got to the other side, one of the other squires grabbed the reins and held Guinevere while Sebastian hobbled over to us. 'Are you all all right in there?' he whispered as he righted us on the saddle and turned the horse around. 'That didn't exactly go to plan.'

'The Night Knight must have deflected our blow,' Pradeep replied.

'Exactly,' Sebastian said. 'Your lance was pointed directly at his head, but the Night Knight changed position and blocked the blow. The water landed on his breastplate, not his visor.'

'We have to try again,' I said.

'Your lance is broken,' Sebastian said, taking the water-pistol lance from us and wedging a new one under the arm of the armour. 'I

borrowed a spare – but it's not rigged for your water-jet plan.' He paused. 'I know you don't want to hear this, but you need to stop and forfeit the contest. Before you get hurt.'

Frankie was thrashing around like crazy in his flagon. 'Calm down, Frankie, or you'll fall out,' I said. But that just made him thrash more.

'Wait. Maybe that's what he wants to do?' Pradeep said. 'To throw himself against the Night Knight's visor and shoot him with water at point-blank range.'

Sebastian lifted our visor and peered in at Frankie. 'He's nodding his head,' he said.

'That is what he wants to do.'

The trumpets sounded for the next round. Sebastian started to say, 'No, it's too risky. You need to forfeit . . . *swishy little fishy . . . swishy little fishy . . .*'

'Frankie!' I whispered. 'Did you just zombify Sebastian so he wouldn't stop you?'

I could feel Frankie nod.

'Maybe this isn't such a good idea . . .' Pradeep began, but Guinevere was already racing down the track.

The hoofs got louder and louder and I remembered the feeling of the lances hitting one another.

'Hang in there, Pradeep!' I cried.

A second later, I heard a whoosh as Frankie flung himself out of the helmet. There was a *thwack* – then the sound of popping and fizzing –

and Guinevere started to slow down.

'It sounds like he made it!' Pradeep cried.

'But is Frankie all right?' I yelled.

The sound of the Night Knight's horse's hoofs got further and further away. Then we heard a big pop like a massive bottle of cola exploding from putting too many mints in it.

'I think that was the Night Knight's circuit board exploding,' Pradeep said.

'It worked,' I cried. 'But we've got to get back and rescue Frankie. How do we get Guinevere to stop?'

CHAPTER 17
RUNAWAY STEED

'I'm not sure Frankie's controlling the horse any more,' Pradeep shouted to me. We were being bounced around as Guinevere turned right, then left, and reared up in confusion.

Suddenly we heard Sebastian's voice echo across the field. 'Guinevere, yield!'

If Sebastian was unzombified too, that could only mean one thing. Frankie must have been knocked out. Or worse . . .

'Good girl,' Sebastian's voice said. Guinevere was immediately calm. 'I've got you, guys,' he added. I could feel a tug on the reins. 'Are you all right in there?'

'I'm OK. Are you, Pradeep?' I asked.

'Urgh . . . I think I feel horse-sick,' he moaned.

'Sebastian, where's Frankie?' I said. 'We need to get him back into water right away!'

'I don't know,' Sebastian said. 'The Knight Night's horse had a bit of a fright when her rider started popping and fizzing. She jumped over the arena barrier and headed for the moat. We can hide behind the stands so I can get you off Guinevere and out of the armour. Then we can look for Frankie together.'

Less than a minute later Sebastian removed the helmet and undid the armour to release me and then Pradeep, who was looking pretty green from the horse-sickness by now. As soon as his feet hit the ground, we raced after the crowd that was heading for the moat, with Sebastian leading Guinevere behind us.

'What hast happened here?' Motley Fool was shouting as we arrived at the drawbridge. We could see the Night Knight sitting in the moat with the water up to his chest. He wasn't moving but a stream of smoke trickled out of his visor. His horse was standing next to him, having a drink.

The medical team from the castle had already waded into the water and were carefully pulling off the Night Knight's helmet. The crowd gasped when they couldn't see a head inside, only a fizzing circuit board.

Motley Fool scratched his head, making his jingly bells jingle even more. 'Those boys and the

Knight-Mare were right!' he muttered to himself.

'I'll see to the Night Knight's horse,' Sebastian shouted, and whistled to her. She calmly walked up the bank and let him take her reins. 'I'll get her back to the stables. Can you keep an eye on Guinevere?' he added as he passed us.

Pradeep nodded while I looked around for Frankie, scanning the water, the bank, the drawbridge, *everywhere*, for a speck of orange. 'He must be in the moat,' I said hopefully.

'Unless he fell out of the visor as the Night Knight rode over here,' said Pradeep. 'Then he could be anywhere.'

Just then we heard little footsteps behind us on the drawbridge. 'Swishy fishy sleepy,' Sami interrupted. 'Look!'

Inside her pointy princess hat was Frankie, floating in some muddy water.

'Where was he, Sami?' I asked.

'Swishy fishy flopping in puddle.' She looked down, 'But then he got sleepy.'

'He needs food,'
Pradeep replied.
Just then
Guinevere nudged
me with her nose.
She was carrying a
paper bag in her teeth.
Inside were her sugar
cube treats. I dropped a couple of green ones into
the water in Sami's hat and Frankie perked up
right away.

'Thank goodness!' I breathed a sigh of relief.

Suddenly Pradeep nudged me – we could see
the top of a pointy hat hidden behind a low wall
nearby. 'Sanj and Mark,' he whispered. We crept
closer.

'So you didn't think to make the mega-robot
waterproof?' Mark shouted.

'I don't see you coming up with any amazing
technological advancements – so you can zip it!'
Sanj shouted back.

'Exactly! A giant zippy bag! How hard would it have been to make a giant waterproof zippy bag for the electric stuff inside the suit!' Mark screamed. 'And I really wanted to take over the world with a bunch of robot knights too. Man! This rots!'

CHAPTER 18

THE KNIGHT OF THE TOURNAMENT

'Wait,' Sanj interrupted Mark's rant. 'The camera! You've been videoing the whole thing. We have proof of the Night Knight's powers *and* we have the blueprints. We can build it *again*. Where is the camera?'

By now we were right next to the wall.

'Ummm . . .' Mark began. 'I videoed the final joust . . . and then when the robot started to smoke and the horse ran off, I put it on my seat under my hat and ran over here.'

Sami peeked over the wall. 'Me got camera!' She smiled and pulled it out of a pocket in her princess outfit.

Sanj and Mark turned to look up at us in surprise.

'No, Sami!' Pradeep shouted. 'They need that to win the *Evil Scientist Magazine* Evil Robot competition!'

'Too late,' Sanj said, jumping up and snatching the camera from Sami's hands.

'Yeah, too bad, morons!' said Mark, and laughed his evil laugh.

Sanj pressed 'play'. Then he froze. 'What is this?' he asked. He held up the camera screen, which was showing a video of Sami fighting pretend dragons with her pointy princess hat. 'Where is the footage of the Night Knight?'

'It was on there!' Mark said. 'I had the arrows

and the boulder and everything.'

'She must have recorded over it.'

'I make movies, yaaaaayyyy!' Sami giggled.

'At least we still have the blueprints,' Sanj muttered.

'About those blueprints,' Sebastian interrupted, walking up to us with Guinevere by his side. 'I found them in the armour that the boys used in the joust.'

'Wait, it was you in the joust just now?' Mark stared blankly at us.

'And Frankie,' Pradeep said as Frankie jumped up out of Sami's hat and splashed Mark in the face.

'Blech!' Mark spluttered.

'The blueprints are with the competition officials now,' Sebastian continued. 'And they *really* want to speak to you about your robot.'

'No way!' Sanj stomped his foot.

'Ah, here they are,' said Sebastian with a

smile, motioning to two burly officials who were walking our way.

'Don't even think about running, Mr Wizard and Lord whatever-your-name-is,' the first official said.

'Let's go and find your parents and have a word, shall we?' said the second. They took Mark and Sanj away, still sniping at each other.

We could see Mrs Kumar hurrying over to the officials. She waved at Pradeep and shouted, 'Pradeep my lovely, look after Sami, will you? Your brother has got himself into a pickle again.'

Motley Fool walked up to join us. 'The Night Knight hath been disqualified. Therefore the honour of Knight of the Tournament falls to you,' he said to Sebastian. He paused and squinted down at me, Pradeep and Sami. 'And your, er . . . squire . . . ?' he trailed off.

Sebastian whispered something to the fool.

'An excellent suggestion,' Motley Fool nodded. 'Let us make haste!'

As we walked back towards the castle courtyard, we bumped into Mrs Richards. She did not have her happy history face on now.

Sebastian stepped forward and grabbed her hand, giving it a kiss. 'Fair lady, thank you so much for letting your students help me . . . er . . . tend to my horse, Guinevere, during this strangest of tournaments. May I borrow them for a few moments more? I am sure they'll have much to tell their class when they return to school.'

Mrs Richards blushed. 'I suppose so. As long as it's historically pertinent.' She swept off to count the rest of the peasants.

'Right, then,' said Sebastian, turning to us. 'Let's get this show on the road.'

As we entered the courtyard the crowd cheered and clapped and the trumpets sounded – but this time we weren't sitting on a wall or stuck in a tower. We were sitting on the back of a tall majestic horse – Sami, Pradeep and me, with

Frankie in Sebastian's helmet filled with water. Sebastian led Guinevere along and she high-stepped proudly through the crowd.

Mrs Kumar was waving to us from the stands, while Sanj and Mark – who were now dressed in medieval prison clothes – stood next to her scowling.

We were so excited that we almost didn't see the ball of fur and claws as it shot through the air, aiming straight for Frankie!

'Fang!' Sami, Pradeep and I all shouted.

But we shouldn't have worried. With one *swish* of her long tail, Guinevere thwacked Fang out

of the way and into a barrel of water next to the medieval prisoners. Mark pulled her

out and dried her on his prison smock. 'This is the worst!' I saw him mutter.

'Raaaaooooowwwwlll,' his soggy moggy mewed back.

When we got to the front of the courtyard, Motley Fool jingled his bells for silence. 'The honour of the Knight of the Tournament is to be bestowed upon Sir Knight-Mare and his squire Pra-tom, who alas can't be here for reasons one doest not fully comprehend,' he shouted. 'In Pra-tom's stead, we have the Knight-Mare's three assistant squires, with their mascot of, er . . . ' He peered into the helmet. 'A golden fish!'

'What do we get?' I whispered to Sebastian. 'A medal?'

'A trophy?' Pradeep asked.

'You'll see.' Sebastian smiled.

Motley Fool reached into a jewelled box in front of him and pulled out . . . a flower! Each of us got a different colour. Apparently that was the custom for tournaments.

Sami seemed pretty pleased with hers.

'Our mums will like them, I guess,' I grumbled to Pradeep. 'But what will Frankie do with his?'

'I don't think we have to worry about that,' Pradeep said as Frankie wiped the last green rose petals from his mouth and let out a satisfied burp. 'I think he likes this kind of reward.'

JURASSIC CARP

CHAPTER 1
A TAIL OF TWO FISH

We sat in the crowded room and waited.

'How long is this talk?' I whispered to my best friend Pradeep.

'You can't possibly be bored!' he whispered back. 'It hasn't even started yet.'

A lady in a white science coat stepped on to the stage in front of the audience. The crowd in the school auditorium started clapping – and she did that weird thing where the person who is being applauded mouths 'Thank you' over and over and bows a little – even though there's a microphone so she could just as easily have said thanks.

'Is she somebody important?' I whispered slightly more loudly.

Pradeep continued clapping as he answered. 'That's Dr Lorna McDoom. Renowned archaeologist and palaeontologist.'

'And *is* she somebody important?' I asked again.

'Do you actually mean, "Did she star in a movie I've seen? A video game I've played? Or invent something I couldn't live without, like cheese puffs?"' Pradeep whispered back.

'Yes,' I answered. 'Did she invent cheese puffs?'

'No,' Pradeep replied,

'but she is really, *really* important in the world of digging up dinosaur bones.'

That, to Pradeep, was the same as saying she was the top of the Premier League for most other kids. 'I get it,' I said. 'I'll shut up.'

Just then the scientist spoke into the microphone. 'Thank you so much for your enthusiastic welcome to Parkside Primary School!' she lilted in a thick Scottish accent. The applause died down and she continued. 'It's a pleasure to be here with you to share this new discovery which I think is truly . . .' She paused.

'EPIC!' the word burst out of Pradeep before he could stop it. His hands clapped over his mouth a second too late and his face turned red as the audience turned to see who had spoken.

'Mwah haa, hee, hee, hee!' Dr McDoom giggled. 'Well, I'll take your word on that, young man.' She smiled at Pradeep. 'Epic,' she repeated.

Pradeep released his mouth and started to breathe again.

'Did you hear her laugh?' I whispered to Pradeep.

'I was concentrating on disappearing into the floor,' he answered. 'So no.'

'It's just . . . she sounded kinda ev—'

'Now,' interrupted Dr McDoom. 'I have some slides to show you that chronicle the excavation of the dig site here on the grounds of this very school.' She squinted into the audience towards the janitor at the back of the hall. 'Could you please turn off the lights?'

The school janitor, who is probably the slowest man in the world (snails on zimmer-frames could actually outrun him), reached for the light switches. Slowly the room started to fade into darkness.

'Any time now, thank you.' Dr McDoom tapped her fingers on the podium. The audience sighed.

Eventually all the lights went out.

'Sorry . . . there's still a green light on in

the audience. Could you turn it off please?' Dr McDoom asked.

It was only then that I realized that Frankie, my pet zombie goldfish, who was hidden in a water bottle on my lap, had popped open the lid to take a look at the slide show. His eyes were glowing a fierce zombie green.

I threw my jacket over the bottle to hide the glow.

'Thank you,' Dr McDoom continued. 'Let's begin.'

While she showed the first couple of slides, Pradeep gave me a look that I thought said, 'Seriously, Tom, why did you buy Frankie a luxury face swill?'

I responded with a look that said, 'A what *what*?'

I squinted through the dark to see Pradeep give me his 'pay attention' look, followed by a look that said, 'Why did you book

Frankie on a luminous fuse crawl?'

'Sorry, what?' I whispered.

'I said, "Why did you bring Frankie to a lecture on fossils"?' Pradeep whispered back.

'*Oh*,' I said out loud. 'That makes much more sense.'

'Shhhhh!' the person behind us tutted.

'Well it's a good thing I did bring him,' I whispered to Pradeep, 'because Frankie obviously senses that something is wrong. His eyes only glow green when he senses danger.'

'He probably just saw the white science coat and thought of Mark,' Pradeep whispered back.

I was about to answer when I realized that Pradeep was probably right. Frankie has *hated* my Evil Scientist big brother Mark ever since he dunked him in toxic gunge and tried to

126

flush him – so it made sense that when he saw a white coat, he would literally go green with anger. Or at least his eyes would.

I looked down and realized that while we were talking, Frankie had chewed a hole in my jacket so he could see out. Mum was going to kill me. She was already mad that there were green food stains on practically everything I wear from scavenging green snacks for Frankie. He has a thing for green food, the grosser and slimier the better.

Frankie's eyes had stopped glowing, but he was definitely still interested in Dr McDoom. The slide she had up on the screen was of a large skeleton, about the size of a small car, that was found under the school car park while they were digging foundations for a new science block. It was definitely a fish. It looked kinda . . . I don't know . . . prehistoric, with big sharp teeth and huge eye sockets.

'With computer modelling and my knowledge

of the fish of this era,' Dr McDoom continued, 'the next slide reveals how we think *this* prehistoric fish, which we believe is from the Jurassic period, would have looked . . .'

The next slide came up and the room went silent.

That is, except for Pradeep and me.

'Frankie?' we both mumbled.

CHAPTER 2
A VERY FISHY PAST

The image on the slide was exactly like a giant, prehistoric version of Frankie, but with a kind of dopey look on his face.

Frankie looked at Pradeep and then at me. Then he did an impression of the dopey prehistoric fish.

'Argh!' I yelled.

Pradeep quickly threw his coat over my holey jacket to hide Frankie.

'Ah-ha!' he shouted and punched the air to cover my yell. 'That is also EPIC!'

Dr McDoom smiled. 'I think so too,' she said.

'I'll take Frankie out before he causes a scene,' I whispered to Pradeep. I stood up and started to make my way to the back of the hall while Dr McDoom kept talking. 'This is, of course, a computer-generated image. But what if it was within our power to make this fish real?'

I could see Pradeep sit up in his seat to listen closer.

'In addition to the bone and rock we found with the specimen, we also found traces of DNA material, that if sequenced and spliced correctly with a host species, could be cloned into a form

of this majestic animal that swam these shores some one hundred and fifty million years ago. The closest living relative to this specimen of prehistoric fish is the common carp or modern goldfish. Just imagine the possibilities if we could bring back an animal that time forgot?'

The audience started to murmur. I don't think they liked the idea of bringing the giant fish back to life and neither did Frankie. He was thrashing around like mad under the jackets, trying to get out of his bottle.

'Of course, I am only speaking hypothetically!' Dr McDoom added.

By now, Pradeep had joined me at the back of the hall. Before I even had a chance to ask, he said, 'It means that she's just asking "What if?" – not that she's actually going to try to do it.'

'Right,' I said, nodding. 'I knew that.'

By now Frankie had chewed through Pradeep's jacket as well as mine and looked ready to jump out of the bottle and throw himself at the projector.

'We better get out of here,' I whispered to Pradeep.

'I just want to hear this end bit,' he said.

'In conclusion, I think we should be opening doors in science, not shutting them.' Dr McDoom pointed to the slide again. 'Even if it means that *this* is what's behind one of the doors.'

She laughed again at her own joke, but this time it was a full 'Mwhaaa haaa haaa haaa!' that my Evil Scientist big brother Mark would have been proud of.

Pradeep and I headed out of the auditorium while everyone clapped. Just as we got to the exit, we looked back and saw Mark approach the stage. What was he doing here at our school? And on a Saturday?

My lip-reading skills are pretty good but from that distance all I could make out was, 'I think we have the same ideas about science. And I

think I know where you can get the perfect . . .'
Then Mark turned away and I couldn't see what
he was saying any more.

Pradeep and I were rushed through the doors
with the rest of the crowd.

'Mark seemed pretty interested in talking to Dr
McDoom,' I said.

'Yeah,' Pradeep admitted.

'And her laugh definitely sounded evil,' I
added.

'But we don't have any proof that she's
actually an Evil Scientist. Even if she *is* talking to
Mark. She's a world-renowned palaeontologist.
We can't just accuse her of being evil just
because she has an evil laugh,' Pradeep defended
her.

'And an evil name,' I said.

Frankie popped his head through the holes in
both jackets and nodded.

'McDoom does sound kind of evil,' Pradeep
admitted.

'*And* the fact that she told everyone that she wants to clone a giant monster version of prehistoric Frankie,' I said. Frankie started to thrash when I said that, so I pushed him back into the bottle and balled up the jackets around it. 'We need to let Frankie work off some steam,' I added.

'We've got some time before we meet Mum and Sami at the school pool for Sami's swim class,' Pradeep said, looking at his watch. 'Maybe we can go to the pool early and let Frankie have some swim time?'

I whispered to the jackets, 'Would you like that, Frankie?' The jackets moved up and down.

'I think that's a yes,' Pradeep said.

'Also, the old lifeguard that works on Saturdays never wears his glasses,' I added. 'He thinks that Frankie is a pool toy. Perfect!'

We walked out of the hall and headed towards the pool. Our swim bags were in our class cupboard in the changing rooms. In no time we were in the water, with the whole place to ourselves, except for the short-sighted lifeguard.

Frankie had a great time. He likes to do zombie-fast laps and play *Jaws*, which is where me or Pradeep lies flat on a float as he swims up from underneath and bumps us off it. He was having such a good time that we left him in the water while we got changed.

But when we went out to scoop him back into his water bottle . . . he was gone!

CHAPTER 3

FISH-NAPPED!

We looked everywhere! In the pile of floats, in
the coil of rope that separates the lanes, even in
the lost-and-found pile of goggles and flippers!
No Frankie.

'Excuse me.' Pradeep poked the lifeguard, who
was having a quick snooze in his chair while the
pool was empty. 'Um . . . our orange pool toy
is missing? Did you see anyone in here after we
left?'

'Wha . . . ? What?' said the lifeguard, waking
up with a snort. 'The pool is not responsible for
any lost items . . .'

'No!' I interrupted. 'It's not that – we just want

to know if you saw anyone else in here?'

The lifeguard frowned. 'There was a boy, bigger than you. With a white jacket. He said he was from the Pool Maintenance department.'

'Mark!' Pradeep and I said together.

'He had a vacuum thing that he used to clean out the pool.' The lifeguard paused. 'Only something seemed to get stuck in it pretty quickly and he had to go off and fix the vacuum.' He scratched his head. 'You could check with the Pool Maintenance Department to see if they found your toy?'

'There is no Pool Maintenance Department!'

I said. Then I turned to Pradeep. 'There isn't a Pool Maintenance Department at our school, is there?'

'There's just the janitor with a sieve on a stick to pick dead bugs out of the pool,' he answered.

'Then that means Mark has Frankie!' I cried.

The lifeguard looked confused.

'That's what we call the pool toy,' Pradeep covered.

'I think I know where we need to start looking,' I added. 'If we can find Dr McDoom, we'll find Mark and Frankie!'

'Look, kids, I hope you find your toy – but do you mind clearing off so I can take a nap before those loud little kids arrive for their lesson?' The lifeguard waved us away and closed his eyes.

We headed straight for the science lab. All of the school buildings were open because of McDoom's talk and the excavation that was still going on in the school's car park.

We crept down the hall in stealth mode –
eyes peeled for Mark or Dr McDoom. As we
approached the lab we could see that the door
was propped open and the lights were on. We
couldn't hear any noise, though, except for
what might be a filter running and the sound of
dripping water.

Pradeep stood on one side of the door and
I stood on the other. I held up my hand and
counted down silently with my fingers until I just
made a fist. 'Is the fist zero?' Pradeep whispered.
'Does that mean go?'

'Yes, that means go,' I whispered back. 'The
fist is always zero.'

'Right,' Pradeep nodded. 'So do we go *now*?'

I sighed. 'If they were in there they would have
heard us by now so let's just walk in.'

Taking a deep breath, I pushed open the door
to the lab and walked in. It was empty.

'Someone's been here recently,' said Pradeep,
scuttling into the room behind me. Inside the

room were lots of strange scientific instruments and computers that weren't there during Friday's science lesson, plus chemicals in test tubes and in specimen jars all over the tables.

Then we spotted the fish tanks.

There were two, side by side. In one the water was murky and it looked like there was a fleck of something golden moving inside – but the water in the other tank had an icy, cloudy, cracked look and . . . it had our missing zombie goldfish inside!

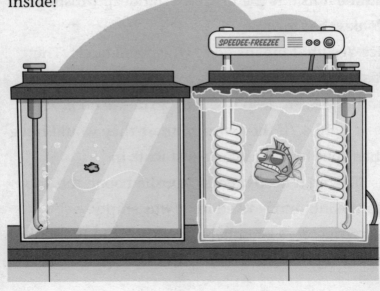

I tapped on the glass. It was freezing cold to the touch. 'Frankie?' I cried. 'It's us! Are you OK? We're here to rescue you.'

Frankie didn't move.

Pradeep touched the tank too. Then he pointed at several tubes inside the tank with Frankie. 'It's not a fish tank,' he said. 'It's a freezer. They've frozen Frankie solid, but why?'

'It doesn't matter!' I cried. 'We've got to get him out!' I managed to find something that looked like a metal skewer and chipped at the ice around Frankie. Luckily, it already seemed to be melting – so it came away without too much trouble. Then I scooped up Frankie, still encased in a football-sized lump of ice, and put him in a glass bowl that Pradeep had found.

Now I know that for any ordinary goldfish, this would be the end of the line. But Frankie has survived loads of times when Mark tried to make him into a frozen fish-pop in our freezer.

'If we can thaw him out, he'll be OK, right?' I asked Pradeep.

'I don't know what they've done to him, Tom.' Pradeep shook his head. 'But we've got to try.'

'Mwaaaah haaa haaa haaa haaa!' an evil laugh came from outside the room, but this laugh was in stereo. At the end we could also here a tiny evil 'Mewwww!'

'That must be Mark and Dr McDoom!' I whispered to Pradeep.

'It sounds like Mark's brought his evil kitten, too!' he muttered back. 'What are we going to do?'

CHAPTER 4
PRE-HISTORIC PRISONER

Pradeep and I had only just managed to hide behind the open lab door when Mark and Dr McDoom walked in. We could just see Fang, Mark's evil vampire kitten, glaring up at Dr McDoom from Mark's Evil Scientist white coat pocket.

'Really, Mark, that went as well as I could have hoped,' Dr McDoom was saying. 'I never could have imagined you would have an ideal host specimen on hand like that.'

'I guess we can get rid of the host-fish thing now?' Mark replied. 'Fang and I can take care of that for you,' and he laughed another evil laugh.

'Och no!' Dr McDoom interrupted. 'Not yet I'm afraid. We need the host fish in case the cloning doesn't take first time. It can be rather tricky.'

They must have looked over at the tanks because the next thing I heard was Mark pounding angrily on a desk. 'The moron fish is gone! I knew I should have fed it to Fang while I had the chance.'

'It *is* disappointing, yes, but that's a wee bit of an overreaction if you ask me,' said Dr McDoom.

Through the crack between the door and doorframe, we could see Fang jump out of Mark's pocket and start licking at the little drips of water that we had left on the floor when we scooped Frankie out of the freezer tank.

Pradeep shot me a look which said, 'If Fang follows the drips . . . they'll lead her straight to us.' I crossed my fingers and toes, and even my eyes, that Fang wouldn't find us. But she kept lapping up the water, getting closer and closer to our hiding place.

'I must say,' said Dr McDoom's voice, 'having a kitten in a sterile laboratory environment is not at all good practice, young man. Especially when the test subjects are fish. Could you please make sure she stays in your pocket and doesn't contaminate any surfaces?'

Mark grumbled and scooped up Fang just before she reached the little puddle dripping from Frankie's bowl and slowly spreading out under the door.

'Pheeew!' Pradeep and I said in looks to each other.

Then Dr McDoom almost squealed in delight. 'Look! Something moved in the cloning tank. Something's moving in there!'

'Hey, RESULT!' Mark shouted, and we heard him tap on the tank.

I peered carefully through the crack. I could see something swimming up to the glass of the murky tank. It looked like a little gold minnow.

I shot Pradeep a look that said, 'That dino-fish has more than doubled in size since we've been here. It's gone from a little gold fleck to a minnow!'

'Doesn't look much like the big fish in the picture,' Mark said.

'It's just started its life!' squealed McDoom in delight. 'We've no idea how big it will get. It's already growing at an unprecedented rate. We'll

have to observe it closely and run some more tests.' She sounded as if she was almost bouncing with excitement. 'I'll need my sequencing calibration instruments from the van. Would you be a pet and help me carry them up here?' Dr McDoom asked Mark. 'We've got a lot of work to do!'

Pradeep and I shrank back against the wall as she raced out of the room, leaving Mark alone.

We heard the sound of him tapping on the tank again. 'Listen up, little dino-fish. If my excellent evil plan has worked, *Dr McDumb* will have no idea that you are not *only* a prehistoric monster fish, but a *zombie* prehistoric monster fish. *You* are going to be my new evil pet and gobble up that nasty little zombie goldfish that belongs to my moron little brother . . . and then . . . well, you can zombify whoever I want – so I can do whatever I want! Got it?'

Just then, Fang belted out a fierce 'HISSSSSS!'

and jumped out of Mark's pocket, clawing at the sides of the fish tank, before bounding out of the room and down the stairs.

'*Oooooh, sensitive!*' Mark smirked as he followed his kitten out of the room.

CHAPTER 5
EXPERIMENT ESCAPE

Pradeep and I waited three whole minutes to make sure the coast was clear, then snuck out from behind the door.

Frankie was mostly thawed out now and beginning to twitch.

'Look, he's moving!' I said.

'Quick, warm him up over here,' Pradeep said, heading for the Bunsen burner. The heat soon turned Frankie's ice block into a watery slush.

Frankie shook off the rest of the ice crystals and high-finned us as we poured him back into his water bottle.

'Phew! It's good to see you back to your

old self, Frankie,' I said.

'And the experiment doesn't seem to have caused any lasting damage,' Pradeep added.

He put Frankie's bottle down next to the murky fish tank while I turned off the Bunsen burner.

'Look,' Pradeep said, suddenly grabbing my arm. 'I think it grew again.'

There in the tank, through the murky water, we could see the eyes of the dino-fish . . . and it was the same size as Frankie!

'Let's get out of here!' I cried. We grabbed Frankie and headed out into the hall. 'We'll take the back stairs. Come on!'

'They used Frankie to clone the dino-fish!' Pradeep wheezed as we clattered down the stairs.

'We've got to tell somebody!' I gasped back. 'That fish could be dangerous. It might have zombie powers like Frankie . . . but even if not –' I gulped – 'do you remember the slide of what it will grow up into?'

'Come on,' Pradeep huffed. 'The Head Teacher and the janitor are probably both still here somewhere. We can take them to the science lab and show them what Mark and Dr McDoom have done!'

We finally found Mrs Prentice, the Head Teacher, in the auditorium, along with the slow-motion school janitor. I actually think a claymation version could move faster.

'Come on!' we kept saying. 'Dr McDoom is doing some really dangerous experiments in the school science lab!'

'I'm sure there is a reasonable explanation for all this,' Mrs Prentice said as she followed us up the stairs. We had to stop every three steps to wait for the janitor to catch up.

'The only reasonable explanation,' Pradeep went on, 'is that Dr McDoom is using an unconventional and highly controversial method of using sampled genetic host materials spliced with harvested prehistoric DNA to create a clone of a Jurassic carp!'

The Head Teacher looked at Pradeep. 'You watch too many science-fiction movies, Mr Kumar.'

Pradeep shook his head in frustration.

'I think what he's trying to say, Mrs Prentice,' I butted in, 'is there is no such thing as too many science-fiction movies for Pradeep.'

Pradeep nodded.

'I just hope that you boys are not wasting our time,' she replied sternly.

We ran the final distance along the hall to the lab and frantically waved them inside. 'Look!' I shouted.

But it was too late. Dr McDoom wasn't there.

Mark wasn't there. But most importantly, the cloned dino-fish wasn't there either. All of Dr McDoom's equipment was gone and the lab was a complete mess. The tank that the dino-fish had been in was smashed to pieces, and there was glass and water all over the floor.

'Oh my word!' Mrs Prentice shrieked as she walked through the door. 'Look indeed!'

'But they were here and the fish was in this tank. It was growing and – and . . .' Pradeep stuttered.

'They must have moved it,' I interrupted.

'Do you know what I think?' Mrs Prentice said coldly. 'I think you boys concocted this ridiculous story to cover up the fact that you were playing in here and broke this fish tank. Destruction of school property, lying, wasting our time,' she continued. 'Ah, there you are, Geoffrey,' she said, as the janitor finally caught up and joined us in the room. 'I'm sorry to say these boys have left the room in a complete mess.'

The janitor grumbled something and started shuffling back out of the room – probably to get a mop.

'At least a week's detention for both of you!' carried on Mrs Prentice. 'I will see both of you after school on Monday. Now – get out of here.'

'But . . . but . . .' I started.

'Come on,' Pradeep said looking at his watch. 'We've got to meet Mum at the pool now.' He turned to the Head. 'I'm sorry we wasted your time, Mrs Prentice. We'll see you in detention.'

As we headed down the stairs I opened Frankie's water bottle. 'Sorry, Frankie, I thought we could stop them.' He patted my arm with his fin. I reached into my pocket and pulled out some old green gummy bears and a bit of pond slime in a zippy bag. 'Here you go,' I said, dropping them into the bottle with him. 'You deserve a treat after all you've been through.'

Frankie gobbled everything down and burped loudly.

'Where could they have moved the fish to so quickly?' I said to Pradeep, wiping the green slime from my hands on my trousers. 'Do you think they realized we were on to them, or do you think they moved it for another reason?'

'I don't know.' Pradeep frowned. 'It could be that McDoom needed to take the fish to another lab . . . but at least we got Frankie back and he seems to be OK.'

By the time we'd got back to the swimming pool, Pradeep's mum was deep in conversation with one of the other parents, so Pradeep and I took Sami, his three-year-old little sister, to get changed before her swimming class started. Sami *loves* seeing Frankie do tricks, so we thought that giving Frankie another dip in the pool would make Sami laugh *and* cheer up Frankie after his morning of being a frozen science experiment.

When Sami was ready, we got her green mermaid rubber swim ring and walked her to the

side of the pool. As the class wasn't due to start
for another ten minutes, the elderly lifeguard
was still having a nap. Quietly I dumped Frankie
into the swimming pool and waited for him
to pop up and do some tricks. But he didn't
reappear.

'Frankie?' I called.

'That's weird,' said Pradeep.

We turned away from Sami just for a second
to scan the pool for Frankie . . . and that's when
we heard the splash.

'Wheeeeee!' Sami squealed as she jumped into the pool with her green rubber ring.

'Sami!' Pradeep shouted to her. 'Paddle to the side! You're not supposed to go in the pool without a grown-up!'

That's when I spotted something orange moving in the water. And it definitely *wasn't* Frankie.

CHAPTER 6

A FISH OUT OF WATER

A large orange fin poked up out of the deep end of the pool, followed by two huge eyes – which were looking right at Sami.

'Sami! Get out now!' I shouted. 'It's the dino-fish!' Pradeep turned to look just as the dog-sized fish started powering towards his sister.

In a second Frankie was in front of the Jurassic carp, blocking its path.

'Zombify him, Frankie!' I called as Pradeep jumped into the water and started dragging Sami to the side of the pool, but the huge fish just reared up and slapped Frankie out of the way with an oversized fin.

'Swishy fishy has fishy friend!' Sami giggled as Frankie flew across the pool. 'Me want to play!'

Pradeep had finally got Sami back to the side of the pool. I knelt down and pulled her out of the water, leaving her green rubber ring floating behind her.

'Pradeep!' I yelled as the dino-fish suddenly charged him. Pradeep turned and shoved the rubber ring between himself and the fish. I could hear a hiss of air . . . the fish's sharp teeth must

have punctured it! Then all of a sudden Frankie
was back. This time, his eyes were glowing a
bright, hypnotic zombie green. He slammed right
into the side of the giant fish, making it drop the
ring and follow him to the other end of the pool.

Pradeep clambered out. A second later
Frankie leaped out of the deep end and on to the
poolside. I ran to get him.

'Are you OK?' I shouted back to Sami and
Pradeep as I scooped up the flailing Frankie and
put him back in his water bottle.

'Fun!' Sami giggled. 'Me play with big swishy
fishy later?'

'I don't think so,' I said, walking back to where
they stood.

'Did you see how big it is now?' Pradeep
gasped. The dino-fish was hiding again in the
deep end of the pool. 'It's the size of a Labrador!'

'Sami Kumar, did you get in that pool without
me there?' Pradeep's mum's voice echoed
through the room.

'Huhhh? What? No, I didn't nod off!' the lifeguard sat up in his chair and looked around.

'Me went swimming with fishies,' Sami cried happily.

'Pradeep, Tom!' Mrs Kumar's shout continued. 'Did you let her go in?'

I quickly shoved the water bottle with Frankie in under my T-shirt.

'We only looked away for a second . . .' Pradeep started.

'Look at the state of you, Pradeep. You're drenched. And look at this swim ring!' Mrs Kumar tutted as she walked towards us, looking at the slowly deflating green ring. 'What will Sami use for swimming class?'

'There won't be a swimming class today.' A Scottish voice rang out as Dr McDoom stepped out of the changing rooms and on to the poolside. 'I'm very sorry but we've had to cancel the classes today to carry out . . . er . . . emergency maintenance on the pool. I'm afraid you all have to leave *immediately*.'

She turned to the lifeguard. 'You can go home now too!' she shouted. The lifeguard practically skipped out of his chair and headed out.

Mrs Kumar wrapped up Sami in a big fluffy towel, handed one to Pradeep and walked us towards the door. Dr McDoom very quickly, but politely, ushered us out of the pool area, waiting while we took all of our things, then exited the pool herself and locked the door behind us. She turned back to make sure we were leaving as she walked across the car park back to the school building.

'I guess we know where they moved the fish!' I whispered to Pradeep.

'And now we know that the fish is definitely dangerous too,' Pradeep said, holding up the rubber ring.

'Now, can I trust you boys to take care of Sami while I go and pull the car around?' Mrs Kumar glared at us. 'And you are soaked, Pradeep!' She huffed. 'It's lucky I always have spare clothes

with me in the car for these situations.'

'Thanks, Mum,' Pradeep said. 'You can trust us to watch Sami.'

I just nodded. A lot. Then we plonked ourselves down on the steps to wait with Sami.

'Miiiaowwww!'

Frankie sprang out of the top of the water bottle at the sound. He looked around, ready for a fight.

'Fang!' Pradeep and I muttered. We turned around to see a very angry-looking Fang wiggling out from a low vent in the pool wall.

'Kitty not happy,' Sami said, and reached out to stroke Fang. Instead of trying to swipe Sami's hand or bite her, Fang rubbed up against Sami's leg and actually let her tickle her.

'That's odd,' I said. 'Fang hates everyone but Mark.'

Even Frankie stood down from his 'on guard' pose and started swimming around his bottle again.

Sami got out her colouring pad and started to doodle. She drew a huge fish with big scary teeth and dopey-looking eyes.

'Look, kitty,' she said, showing Fang the drawing. 'New big swishy fishy!'

Fang extended her claws and with one clean slice she cut the picture in half.

'Ah!' I said, suddenly under-standing. 'I don't think Fang likes the dino-fish either.'

CHAPTER 7

NEVER TRUST A VAMPIRE KITTEN

Suddenly we heard a key in the lock of the
swimming-pool door behind us. Frankie's eyes
started glowing again so I quickly covered him
up with Pradeep's towel.

'I thought the place was empty,' I whispered.
'Quick, let's hide!' We ran down the wooden
steps and hid underneath them, peeking out
through the gaps between the stairs.

The door opened above us and Mark's trainers
appeared on the top step before vanishing again.
Then there was the sound of something heavy
being wheeled over our heads and we saw Mark
pushing a large tank down the wheelchair

ramp from the pool entrance.

'Miaow!' Fang raced out from our hiding place and tried to rub against Mark's leg as he walked.

'Hey, Fang, cut it out!' Mark said, pushing her off to the side with his foot just as Dr McDoom pulled up in her van.

'We'd better get our wee fishy out of here before he outgrows this tank too!' Dr McDoom said as they wheeled the tank round to the back of the van. 'He's a truly wonderful specimen. Mesmerizing, you might say!'

'You can say that again!' said Mark. 'Maybe we should feed it something? Like . . . oh, I dunno . . . maybe something *green*? And have you . . . er . . . checked the fish's eyes?'

We could just make out Dr McDoom staring deep into the dino-fish's eyes, which remained very much *not* green and *not* swirly. She definitely didn't start mumbling 'swishy fishy' or whatever the prehistoric version of that would be. 'Uggy uggy' maybe?

'You're right,' she said to Mark. 'Maybe the not-so-little dear is hungry. I'll get him some dehydrated protein and vitamin food for the ride.'

'Some *what*?' Mark asked.

'Fish flakes,' she said. 'Come on.'

As the van pulled away and we came out from our hiding place, Fang slinked out from under a bush next to the wheelchair ramp.

'We've got to follow them!' Pradeep said.

'We could never keep up on our bikes – besides we have to keep an eye on Sami,' I replied. 'If only we knew where they were heading!'

Fang sauntered up to us and dropped a piece of paper at our feet.

Pradeep picked it up. 'Reservoir Water Sports Centre,' he read. It had a picture of a bunch of kids riding on a banana boat on the front.

'That's where they're going!' I said. 'What's a reservoir anyway?'

'It's a manmade body of water. Like a lake,'

Pradeep answered. 'You know, it might make sense to take the fish there. It's big but it's contained, so the fish can't get out into the rivers or the sea. But why should we trust Fang? It might be a trap.'

Mark's evil kitten glared at us, then slinked over to Sami, who was still holding her torn drawing of the dino-fish. Fang grabbed the picture with her teeth, threw it into the air and kitten-claw-shredded it into confetti.

'Paper snow!' giggled Sami.

'Fang REALLY hates that fish, doesn't she?' Pradeep said.

I nodded. 'Just like you, right, Frankie?' I added, removing Frankie's water bottle from under Pradeep's towel.

Frankie popped his head out and shot a jet of water at Fang. She hissed back at him and tried to lunge for the bottle but I pulled it away.

'Yikes!' I cried. 'Looks like she still hates Frankie too. Let's not get too cosy with the evil kitten just yet.'

Just then we heard the *Booooobeeeeep* of Pradeep's mum's car horn. She has the only car I know that has a horn that sounds like it's shouting, 'Cooooeeeee!'

She pulled into the driveway and handed Pradeep a bag of clothes. He climbed into the back of the car to put them on while she got Sami's things together.

'Muuuummmm!' I could hear Pradeep whine from the back seat. 'These are the clothes that Grandma sent over last year! I thought you gave them away?'

'You mean you thought you got rid of them?' Pradeep's mum said. 'I found the bag you stuffed under your bed, young man.'

'Urgh,' Pradeep groaned.

When he came out he was dressed in a matching T-shirt and shorts decorated with kissing pandas and glittery cupcakes. If a more embarrassing set of clothes existed they would have to be quarantined.

Even Frankie hung his head in shame.

Pradeep shot me a look that simply said, 'Don't.'

While Pradeep's mum was putting Sami into the car I said, 'Um, Mrs Kumar. Sami looks really disappointed that she didn't get to swim.'

I looked over at Sami, who was smiling and not looking disappointed at all. I coughed noisily and added, 'Yep, she looks *really* SAD about it.'

Sami finally understood what I meant and put on her patented 'sad toddler with wobbly bottom lip' face. It's a classic!

'Oh dear,' Mrs Kumar said when she looked at Sami.

'Maybe you could go here?' I said, handing her the flyer that Fang had given us. 'It's supposed to be really fun. We could ride our bikes over and meet you there. Right, Pradeep?'

Pradeep looked up from the kissing pandas on his shirt and nodded. 'Uh huh.'

'Well, I've got to run some errands first, but I suppose we could come later on,' said Mrs Kumar. 'You both be careful. Stick to the cycle paths. And no swimming until I get there!' She wagged her finger at us and we both nodded.

'Right, let's go!' I cried as the car drove off. 'We've got a doctor to see about a dino-fish.'

'I can't go out in public in this!' Pradeep said as we crossed the path to the bike shed.

'You *have* to,' I replied. 'It's for the good of science.' It was low blow but I knew it was the only thing that Pradeep couldn't resist.

'OK,' he mumbled and lifted his glittery-cupcake shorts leg over his bike. 'For science.'

CHAPTER 8
RESERVOIR FISH

The reservoir isn't far from our school but it is pretty isolated. You have to drive down a loooooong driveway to get to it. Then, when you're about to turn back because you think you've got lost, you finally see a sign advertising the water sports centre.

By the time we'd arrived, my back was sore from Frankie thrashing about in his water bottle in my backpack, trying to get out. He was really worked up. I think I got the better deal though, because Pradeep had to take Fang on his bike, which meant he had needle-sharp kitten claws digging into his legs every time they went around a tight corner or over a bump.

'Ooooh, my thighs,' Pradeep moaned as he carefully got off his bike at the water sports centre. Fang leaped down and immediately ran off towards Dr McDoom's van.

We locked up our bikes and I opened the lid of Frankie's water bottle to let him peek out. He poked his head out as far as it would go and strained to see if he could spot any sign of Mark, Dr McDoom or the dino-fish. Then he motioned with his fin and pointed.

Pradeep and and I followed his fin. We could just make out someone in a white scientist coat standing in front of the van by the water's edge in a small roped-off area of the reservoir. There were large wind buffers, like fences, blocking our view, so we couldn't see what was in the water.

'Mark!' Pradeep and I said at the same time.

The reservoir itself was massive. It was the size of at least two football pitches, and kind of bean-shaped. We were at one end of the bump and

Mark was in a corner of the opposite end. The motorboats and banana boats were all moored up on the far side of the lake. There were some other people at our end parking their cars and vans, but they didn't look like they were here for water sports. On the other side of the car park Dr McDoom was speaking to some people with microphones and cameras. There were other people in white coats there as well.

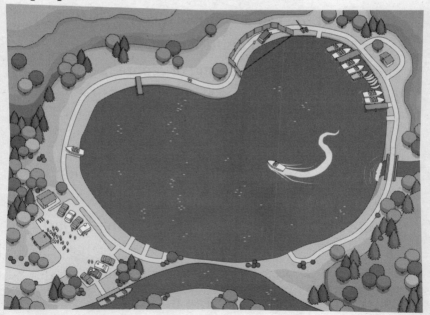

'In good time, people.' She held up her hands. 'We have some final arrangements to make and then we shall make the announcement you've been waiting to hear.'

'She's going to show them the dino-fish!' I said. 'That must be her plan.'

'And if it *is* a giant zombie fish, Mark will be able to make it zombify all the reporters to do whatever he wants,' Pradeep said. 'We still don't know what the fish is capable of!'

Dr McDoom didn't notice us as we sneaked through the throng of reporters and headed towards Mark at the far end of the lake. When we got close enough we hid behind the van so we could see Mark without being seen. Fang had followed us but I couldn't see any sign of her now. That worried me. You should always know where an evil kitten is, *just in case*.

'I know you've got some zombie fish in you!' Mark was saying – pointing into the roped-

off section of the reservoir. 'There are lots of people coming to see you . . . and you are going to hypnotize them and put them under my control. Then I'll have a team of scientists that I can turn evil, and reporters to tell the world all about the cool evil stuff that we're gonna do. This is going to rock. And why are you going to do this for me, my wittle-evil dino-fish? Cos I'm the person with the yummy green treats, aren't I?'

He held up a mouldy green piece of bread high above his head and the fish jumped clear out of the water, and snapped it out of Mark's hand.

Pradeep and I gasped. The dino-fish was now the size of a small whale!

Frankie popped his head out of the water bottle. His eyes were a blazing zombie green but he was also drooling. I don't think he knew if he was angry or hungry or both.

'Hey, mind the nails, fish!' Mark huffed.

'That fish is the size of a car!' I whispered to Pradeep. 'How did it grow so fast?'

'Genetic programming? Accelerated hormone boosting? Intensive thermo-reactive expansion therapy?' Pradeep thought out loud. 'Or maybe it's just big boned?'

'Whatever the reason,' I replied, 'we've got to stop Mark!'

Pradeep pointed. 'Oh no – Frankie! He must be trying to stop Mark on his own!'

 I peered around the edge of the van and saw Frankie jumping from puddle to puddle across the paving towards the water's edge.

Just as Mark tossed the last piece of mouldy green bread into the air over the water, Frankie leaped out over the reservoir and gulped it down in one before splashing into the water.

'Or he just wants food!' I mumbled.

'Hey! Moron fish!' Mark shouted. 'Now you're gonna get it.'

Frankie surfaced from the water, his eyes a full-on zombie green.

'Dino-fish! Sick 'em!' Mark shouted.

CHAPTER 9

GREEN-EYED MONSTER

Pradeep and I ran out from behind the van.

'Swim, Frankie! Swim!' I shouted – as the huge dino-fish surfaced behind him.

'Little morons!' Mark smirked. 'Good. You get to be here to see my evil plan go global. Dr McDoom and I are going to be invited to take this dino-fish all over the world, and wherever we go we can get the fish to zombify people. And if people don't like it . . . well, the dino-fish has a *nasty bite*.'

You won't get away with this!' Pradeep shouted.

'Yeah, I think we will,' Mark said. 'Me and Dr McDoom will be the best evil team ever.'

THE REKNOWNED REGULAR ROUND-UP OF WRONGDOING

EVIL SCIENTIST

Special Report:
Evil Duo Win Again!
PLUS
• Best Budget Dungeons
• Flying Monkeys tested

'Hang on,' I interrupted. 'You've got an Evil Scientist crush on Dr McDoom?!'

'Do not!' Mark shouted.

'Do so,' I said.

'DO NOT!' Mark stomped.

'Do soooooo,' I teased.

We were interrupted by frantic splashing from the water, where Frankie and the dino-fish were circling each other.

'Oh, sorry, Frankie,' I said. 'Come on, jump out of there!' But every time Frankie went to move, the dino-fish was there first.

'Frankie!' Pradeep shouted. 'Try to swim out to the main bit of the reservoir! You'll have a better chance of losing him in a bigger space!'

'He can't.' Mark smiled. 'There's a net stretched under that rope that seals off this whole corner of the lake. It's a protected holding pen. Nothing can get in or out.'

'Unless someone or *something* used a super-sharp cutting device to slice through the rope holding up the net and let the fish out,' Pradeep said.

'Yeah, I guess . . .' Mark sounded confused. 'But who's gonna do that?'

'Um . . . Fang . . . I think,' I mumbled, pointing to the kitten perched at the side of the lake, her razor sharp claws poised to cut the rope.

'Noooooo!' Mark shouted as his kitten swiped her razor-sharp claws downward. 'You can't let the dino-fish free! It'll ruin all our evil plans!'

But he was too late. The rope split in two,

dropping the net to the lake floor.

Both Frankie and the dino-fish stopped
thrashing about in the water and looked out at
the rest of the lake. Then Frankie's eyes dimmed
from their luminous green to their normal
goldfish colour. The huge dino-fish looked right
into Frankie's eyes . . . and for a moment it
looked like the two of them were communicating
in looks. But the moment didn't last long. Fang

leaped from the lakeside directly on to the dino-fish's back. She dug her teeth into its dorsal fin and it reared up in pain, before disappearing under the water with Fang still desperately hanging on to its back.

The water looked eerily still.

'Fang!' Mark yelped, suddenly panicked. 'Where is she?'

It seemed like ages before the dino-fish surfaced again in the main part of the reservoir. It was hidden by the windshields from the growing group of people at the far end of the lake.

'She's there!' Pradeep shouted, and pointed to the wet kitten still clinging to the back of the giant fish. The dino-fish reared up again and Fang fell helplessly into the water.

'I'm coming for you, Fang!' Mark yelled as he pulled off his trainers and dropped his Evil Scientist white coat to the ground. He dived into the water and headed straight for his flailing kitten.

'Mark!' I shouted. 'Be careful!'

But once again the lake was still and the giant fish was nowhere to be seen.

In seconds Mark was with Fang. He scooped her up and put her on his head so she was out of the water. 'I've got muddy water in my eyes,' he gurgled. 'I can't see which way to swim!'

'Hang on, Mark,' I shouted. I grabbed one of the life rings that hung by the waterside and threw it as hard as I could. It got kind of near Mark but not close enough to grab. 'I'm going to have to jump in,' I said to Pradeep.

CHAPTER 10
CAT-ASTROPHE

Just as I started to take off my trainers Pradeep
pointed again. 'Look! It's Frankie.'

Frankie's eyes were glowing again. We could
just see him in the murky water, swimming out
and under the ring and then dragging it over
to Mark. Mark put the ring around himself and
then he paddled, and Frankie pulled them back
to the side of the lake.

I scooped Fang off Mark's head and Pradeep
wrapped her in his jacket to warm her up. Then I
put Mark's Evil Scientist coat over his shoulders.
He sat on the ground as Pradeep handed Mark
the jacket with Fang balled up inside.

'You stupid crazy evil kitten,' Mark said stroking her head. 'What did you do that for? You're the best evil pet in the world. No stupid fish could replace you.'

Fang mewed gently and rubbed her head against Mark's hand. Then she bit him hard on his finger and slashed at Pradeep's jacket to get free. 'OW!' yelled Mark. 'Yup, that's my little evil kitteny-witteny.'

Fang shook out the water from her fur and crept over to where Frankie was panting in a puddle of water inside the life ring.

'Watch out—' I started to say, but instead of attacking him, Fang coughed up the most disgusting green slimy pond scummy hairball I've ever seen and nudged it with her nose towards Frankie.

'He's not really gonna—' Pradeep started to say, before Frankie gulped it down in one and burped a satisfied burp at Fang. 'That is the most *revolting* peace treaty I've ever seen,' he added.

'He *is* a zombie goldfish,' I said. 'They're not known for their table manners.'

Just then, Dr McDoom strode over to the holding area and looked at the scene.

Her evil assistant was soaking wet and sitting on the floor next to a goldfish in a life ring and a very wet and grumpy kitten. Oh yeah, and me and Pradeep were trying to look like all this was perfectly normal.

'Hi, Dr McDoom,' Pradeep said, using his best 'talking to a teacher' voice.

'Don't you "Hi, Dr McDoom" me. What's going on?' She said. 'Wait, you're the boys from the swimming pool? What are you wearing?' she added as Pradeep's glittery cupcake-and-panda outfit sparkled in the sun. 'Wait, and that's the host specimen, isn't it?' She looked around and saw that the rope that was supposed to be holding up the barrier net had been shredded. 'Mark, what on earth happened? Where is our "special discovery"?'

Mark stood up. 'It's out there.' He pointed at the reservoir. 'The stupid moron dino-fish nearly killed Fang.'

'He was provoked,' Pradeep added.

Mark glared at Pradeep.

'The dino-fish can't be announced to the world!' I stood in front of Dr McDoom. 'We won't let you use that fish to carry out any more of your evil plans!'

McDoom threw her head back and laughed a full-on Evil Scientist 'Mwhaaa haaa haaa haa haa!'

'My . . . mwhaaa . . . evil . . . mwhaaaa . . . plans?' she gasped between laughs. 'What on earth are you . . . mwhaa haa haa haa . . . talking about?'

'We know you're an Evil Scientist,' Pradeep said.

'But what could possibly have made you think that?' Dr McDoom wheezed, her laugh finally under control.

'Well . . . there's the white coat,' I said.

'Doctors wear white coats too,' she said. 'Are they evil?'

'And the evil laugh?' Pradeep said with a frown.

'Och! That's just the way I laugh. You should have heard my nanna. She sounded like a proper fairy-tale witch when she heard a good joke.' Dr McDoom smiled. 'What else?'

'Well . . . there's your name,' I said. 'McDoom is pretty evil-sounding, don't you think?'

'Totally,' Mark said. 'But . . . like . . . in a good way.' Fang hissed up at Dr McDoom.

'It's an old highland family name. From the

clan McDoom. It goes back centuries. Ach, is that all you've got?' She put her hands on her hips.

'That and the fact that you've been working with Tom's Evil Scientist big brother, you fish-napped our pet goldfish to experiment on him, and you created a car-sized monster dino-fish which you're going to use to take over the world,' Pradeep said. 'But mostly the other stuff.'

Dr McDoom looked over at Mark and raised an eyebrow, 'You've been pulling my leg then, young man.'

Mark looked down at the floor.

'You lied and said the fish was yours when it was really the pet of these two wee boys,' she said sternly and quietly. 'You really want to be an Evil Scientist . . . not a research scientist. And you want to use the prehistoric fish I cloned to take over the world!'

Mark kept staring at the floor. '*Maybe?*' He shrugged.

'Yeah, he did.' Pradeep and I nodded.

'Miiiaowwww,' Fang agreed.

'I'm so sorry, boys!' Dr McDoom said, turning to us. 'I had no idea.' She crouched down and looked at Frankie swimming around in the puddle inside the life ring. 'I'm sorry, little fishy. I shouldn't have used your genetic material without your permission. I shouldn't have frozen you, and I'm glad to see you have survived unscathed.'

Then she looked back at us. 'But I'm not evil. I just wanted to show the scientific world what was possible. You see, I believe if we are better able to understand the wildlife of the past, we'll be better prepared help the wildlife of the present.'

'But what really happened was you made a giant, scary fish, and no one knows what to do with him!' Pradeep said.

'Where is the fish now!' Dr McDoom suddenly

said, snapping to attention. 'He can't look after himself. We need to find him.'

'I think I know a way,' I said, and looked down at Frankie.

CHAPTER 11
FISHY-FRIEND OR FIEND

Just then we heard a completely familiar but completely unexpected sound.

'Heeelllllooo, loovvveeellyyy!' Pradeep's mum called across the water. Sami's backpack bounced behind her as she skipped towards us in her swimsuit and her taped-up green rubber ring.

'Mum?' Pradeep mumbled.

'Sorry my errands took me so long,' she said, and then she gave Pradeep a big and embarrassing hug. 'You look so cute in Granny's outfit.'

As she pinched his cheeks Pradeep mumbled, 'Muuuum. Not in front of the scientist. Please.'

I was right in the middle of giving Pradeep a look that said, 'Wow, shame about your mum giving you a mega-embarrassing hug,' when Mrs Kumar grabbed me and hugged me too.

'I could get Granny to send over a T-shirt for you too, Tom,' she cried. 'Then you boys could match.'

Mark burst out laughing and Fang even sniggered a little 'Mmmeeew, meeww, meeww!'

Dr McDoom stepped forward. 'Hello, I'm Dr McDoom. We met earlier at the school.' She shook Mrs Kumar's hand. 'Mark, why don't you take Fang and get dried off while we figure out what to do about . . .' She paused. 'Our little problem.'

Mark picked up Fang, still sniggering as he headed off towards the van.

'Your son and his friend were just about to help me with a little science project,' Dr McDoom went on. 'Would it be all right if I borrowed them for a wee while?'

'Me help too?' Sami jumped up and down.

'All right, you can stay with Pradeep and Tom but no going in the water,' Mrs Kumar said. 'I'm going to go over and see what all the fuss is, over by that stage at the other end of the lake.'

As soon as Mrs Kumar was gone I turned to Dr McDoom. 'Sami has a kind of special connection with our pet goldfish,' I told her. 'I *think* she'll be able to help us.'

I scooped up Frankie into his water bottle and handed it to Sami. She stared into his glowing

green eyes and a
moment later she
was staring up
Pradeep's left
nostril with
one eye and
at the side of
the van with the
other.
'Did that goldfish

just hypnotize that little girl? Extraordinary!' Dr McDoom stared at Sami and Frankie.

'Swishy little fishy,' Sami mumbled. Then she got a strange look on her face . . . as if she was talking to Frankie in her head.

'Swishy fishy can't understand big swishy fishy talk,' she said. 'Big fishy talk in pictures. And "uggy uggy" sounds. No words.'

Sami pulled her crayons and paper out of her backpack and started drawing really fast. It looked like a cave painting – but of us and the dino-fish!

'Amazing! She's using prehistoric pictorial communication techniques to interpret for the fish,' Dr McDoom said, looking closely at Sami's drawing.

Pradeep looked over at me and was just about to translate the science language when I said, 'Sami is drawing what the fish has to say, right?'

'Exactly,' he said with a grin.

Sami drew a picture of the dino-fish looking
sad in a box. Then she drew another picture of
him looking happy in big blue space. Finally she
drew a green rubber ring, green seaweed and
Frankie's green zombie eyes, and a picture of the
dino-fish licking his mouth like he was hungry.

'So the dino-fish wants to eat green things.
Like Frankie,' Pradeep said. 'That must be why
he tried to get Sami's green rubber ring. He

wasn't trying to eat her, just the ring.'

'And that must be why the dino-fish only chased Frankie when his eyes were glowing green. He must have thought he was food!' I added.

Sami blinked several times and shook her head. 'All done!' she said, and smiled.

Frankie broke off eye contact and dropped back into his water bottle with a splash.

'Was your goldfish just . . . talking through her?' Dr McDoom sat down on the side of a fence and scratched her head.

'I wouldn't want that moron fish in my head.' Mark smirked as he walked up to us, drying his hair with a towel.

Frankie glared at Mark.

'I think the feeling is mutual,' Pradeep said.

'Frankie and the dino-fish *did* look like they were communicating in looks before the dino-fish swam off with Fang. That must have been when Frankie found out all that stuff!' I said.

Dr McDoom looked out at the water in the reservoir and then over at Sami. Then she turned and looked at all the reporters and scientists gathered for her announcement. 'I can't do it,' she said. 'I can't subject the dino-fish to a life in a tank being poked and prodded . . . but I can't just let him loose either.'

Sami tugged on the hem of Dr McDoom's white coat. 'Dino-fishy need babysitter?' she asked.

Dr McDoom smiled down at Sami. 'That's exactly right!' she said. 'If I can follow the dino-fish in the wild I can look after it and also study its behaviour.'

'So . . . no taking over the world? No evil plans at all?' Mark grumped. 'Oh, man!' Fang sat smugly in Mark's pocket sharpening her claws on her teeth.

'Now, Mark, I'm counting on you to help with this,' Dr McDoom said.

'Oh come on!' Mark groaned as Fang jumped

out of his pocket, hissed and started drawing
with her paw in the dirt.

'I think your evil kitten is giving you an
ultimatum, Mark,' Pradeep said.

'A what?' he said.

'She's saying it's the dino-fish or her,' I said.

Fang mewed and nodded.
We looked down at her
drawing. It was a fish with
a big cross through it.

'OK, OK, I'll help
get rid of the dino-
fish.' Mark sighed, and
Fang jumped back
into his pocket,
purring loudly.

'Dr McDoom,'
Pradeep said. 'I think I
have an idea for how you can escape
with the dino-fish *and* avoid all the reporters
and scientists.'

'We're going to need Frankie to do some acting for this one, right?' I added.

'Oh, yeah,' Pradeep said. 'Frankie, can you do your dino-fish face again?'

Frankie did the same expression as when Dr McDoom first showed the slide of the dino-fish in the school auditorium.

'Amazing,' breathed Dr McDoom. 'That's one very special goldfish you have there. OK, boys, let's get to work!'

CHAPTER 12
FRANKIE IN THE SPOTLIGHT

The first thing we needed to do was get the dino-fish in on our plans. Frankie jumped into the water and turned up the green brightness of his eyes as high as he could. In a flash the dino-fish was there. Frankie quickly let his eyes return to normal while Sami drew pictures of the plan and showed each of them to the giant fish.

'Dino fishy like pictures,' Sami said. She patted the enormous fish on the head. With a splash the dino-fish lifted up his front fin and patted Sami on the head in return.

'And he learns fast, too,' Pradeep said. 'Are you ready, Frankie?'

Frankie turned and gave us a fins-up sign.

Next, we scooped Frankie back into his bottle so he could zombify Sami again. If everything went to plan, she would hopefully be able to communicate a little bit with the dino-fish in her head.

Finally, behind the cover of the giant windshields, Frankie jumped into the enormous tank that Dr McDoom had ordered to transport the dino-fish to the stage area, which was then covered with a large black sheet. A mobile crane that was normally used for moving boats picked up the tank and rolled slowly towards the stage at the far end of the lake.

Before she walked over to the stage, Dr McDoom gave us a pair of binoculars and some clip-on microphones and earpieces so she could communicate with us.

'I use these for my public speaking engagements all the time,' she said. 'But I never thought they would come in useful for secret escape plans!' She smiled and allowed herself a little 'Mwhhaa haa hee hee' laugh. 'This is exciting, really.'

The cameras were all switched on and the reporters stood at the ready as the crane put the tank in place and Dr McDoom took to the stage.

Meanwhile, we had to get the dino-fish across the entire length of the reservoir while the press conference was going on – without being seen. At the far end there was only a metre or so of land between the reservoir and a local river that then led out to sea.

'The best way to be unseen is actually to be seen,' Pradeep said.

'Hunh?' Mark, Sami and I said at the same time.

'What if we ride the dino-fish across the reservoir?' Pradeep smiled.

'I knew all your smart brain cells would dry up eventually. You've totally lost it,' Mark said.

Then a little light bulb went off in my brain.

I took the water sports centre flyer that Sami was still gripping in her hand and looked at the picture of the kids on the banana boat on the front.

'Pradeep's a genius!' I said. 'No one will look at what we're riding! They'll just see some happy kids having a ride at the water sports centre!' I held up the picture.

'When you're talking to the dino-fish in your

head, Sami, remember to think in pictures,'
Pradeep said.

'Me picture riding in water!' Sami giggled. She
looked over at the dino-fish, who was swimming
in circles in the water. 'Big swishy fishy boat ride.
Wheeeeeee!'

CHAPTER 13

THIS PLAN IS BANANAS

'I don't know why I agreed to do this,' Mark huffed as he sat behind the controls of a motorboat at the edge of the water. Fang sat by the steering wheel washing her paws.

'Because if you don't, Dr McDoom said she would tell Mum about all your lies and you'll be grounded forever,' I said.

'Oh yeah,' Mark said. 'That.' He started the engine.

Pradeep, Sami and I all climbed on to the back of the dino-fish and he started to swim.

'Sami, keep think-talking to the dino-fish so he knows what to do, OK?' I said.

'Wheeeee! Swishy fishy fun,' Sami said in a half-zombie kind of way.

Mark gunned the engine and sped away from the shore, and the dino-fish followed, close enough so it looked like we were being towed by the motorboat. We must have looked just like the kids on the picture.

Mrs Kumar, who was in the audience, along with lots of the reporters and scientists, waved to us as we passed the stage. They all assumed it was part of the build-up to the announcement, I guess.

With my lip-reading I could tell that Mrs Kumar said to the man next to her, 'My children are on that banana boat. Apparently this is part of a science project! Dr McDoom specifically asked them to help, you know.' She paused and shook her head. 'Science certainly has changed since I was at school.'

By the time Dr McDoom started to speak we had pulled up to the shore at the other side of the reservoir, as close to the river as we could get. The dino-fish let us off his back and swam nearby as we stood on the shore next to where Mark had parked the motorboat. We could hear what Dr McDoom was saying via the radio mics she had given us.

'Friends and colleagues,' she began. 'I think it is time for science to open new doors. To take chances and risks that will lead to exiting new discoveries.'

The crowd applauded.

'I have here the results of my experiments. My very exciting discovery that will change the way we look at palaeontology and genetics forever . . .'

With that the curtain lifted and the contents of the tank were revealed.

Instead of the gasp of awe that might have happened if they'd actually been shown the real dino-fish – what happened next was more of a rumble of confusion.

Mumbles of 'Hunh?', 'Wha?' and 'I need my glasses to see that' filled the crowd.

I suppose Frankie was swimming about in the tank doing his best impression of the dino-goldfish face, so basically looking kinda dopey and confused.

'Ummmm, it looks like an ordinary goldfish?' came the voice of what I guessed was one of the reporters.

'Does it?' Dr McDoom asked.

'It doesn't look anything like the image of the

fish that you showed us at your talk at the excavation site this morning,' another voice said.

'No, I suppose it doesn't,' Dr McDoom replied.

The reporters all started mumbling about having their time wasted.

'Not the front page news we were after,' said one voice.

'Yeah, I'll be lucky if this gets a mention in the paper at all,' grumbled another.

'This is exactly what we were hoping for,' Dr McDoom whispered into the mic under her breath. 'OK, Mark, you can drop the boat back now,' she added.

'This totally ends me helping you now, morons,' Mark said as he started up the motor. 'It's me and Fang back to normal evil business as usual – right, Fang?'

Fang hissed at us as the boat sped away towards the stage.

I looked through the binoculars at the stage

where Dr McDoom was standing with some other scientists.

'Dr McDoom?' one of them said to her. 'We're worried that you've been under too much stress with this project. Have you thought about taking a break?'

'Take a rest from your research for a bit,' another voice said. 'You'll come back to it refreshed in a year or . . .' He trailed off.

'Maybe in two or three years?' another voice chipped in.

'You know,' Dr McDoom said. 'That's exactly what I was thinking.' She took a specimen jar out of her pocket and leaned over the tank with Frankie in it. 'I think I'll take him with me to keep me company,' she said, scooping him up. Then she walked over to the side of the lake where Mark had just pulled up in the motorboat.

'Thanks, Mark,' she said, getting behind the controls while Mark and Fang climbed ashore. 'You know . . .' She paused. 'You are a really good scientist. If you ever decide to stop specializing in evil science, let me know and I'll try to get you some work experience in a non-evil lab.'

'Cool,' Mark said. 'I'm good with the evil stuff for now though, but thanks for asking.' They both laughed a loud 'Mwhaaa haaa haaa haa'. Then Dr McDoom pulled away from the side of the bank and drove the motorboat back towards the dino-fish.

CHAPTER 14
A FISHY NEW CHAPTER

As Dr McDoom's boat pulled up, the wake splashed over our feet and the dino-fish circled the boat, zooming around and bouncing on the waves.

'Big swishy fishy want to play more,' Sami said.

'And I hope that's what he'll get the chance to do,' Dr McDoom said as she stepped off the boat. 'I can take the next few years to just observe and study the dino-fish in its natural environment. I'll get to see him eat and play, and possibly see how he interacts with other animals!'

Frankie jumped up out of the specimen jar in her hand and splashed into the water. 'There's one animal he already seems to have developed a relationship with!' She smiled as Frankie and the dino-fish played chase.

'I'm sorry that we, umm . . . you know, thought you were . . . evil,' I mumbled.

'Yes, I will never judge someone on their evil name and evil laugh again,' Pradeep added.

'That's all right.' Dr McDoom smiled. 'Thank you, boys. Oh and please apologize to your school on my behalf as well. We left so quickly that we left your school lab in a wee bit of a state.' She handed Pradeep a letter addressed to the head teacher. 'This explains what happened and also has a cheque enclosed to pay for any damage. I hope it will prevent any bad feelings.'

'It will definitely prevent a week of bad detentions for us!' Pradeep answered. 'Thanks.'

'And thank you, Sami, for helping me to realize what was best for the dino-fish, and for me too.' Dr McDoom splashed the water with her hand and the dino-fish poked his head out.

'I think we'd better head out to the river before anyone wanders over to take a closer look,' she said to the giant fish.

Frankie popped his head out of the water too and Sami scooped him up in her cupped hands. She immediately got the zombie stare.

Pradeep grabbed Frankie while Sami took out her crayons and paper and speedily drew a big fish playing with a little fish. Then she drew the big fish swimming away and a tear in the big fish's eye.

I looked up from the drawing to the dino-fish. I could swear he looked sad. Not that you can really tell when a giant fish is frowning, what with all the scales and teeth and stuff, but his eyes looked sadder.

Then Sami added another cave drawing of me and Pradeep and Sami, but with fins.

'Do you think that's supposed to be us?' Pradeep asked.

Sami added some pandas and cupcakes to Pradeep's top in bright pink crayon.

'That's definitely us,' I replied.

Pradeep leaned out over the water and stroked the dino-fish behind the gills, just the way that Frankie likes. The dino-fish rolled over on his side and kind of fish-purred.

Dr McDoom had got out a notebook and was scribbling in it. 'Very interesting,' she mumbled.

'Goodbye, dino-fish,' I said, patting him on the head. 'I hope you find lots of yummy green food out in the big water.'

He rolled back over and splashed his tail, soaking us all.

'I guess I'll have to get used to that,' Dr McDoom said, shaking water off her shoes.

Sami snapped out of her zombie trance. She

smiled at the dino-fish, took her green crayon out and held it out. 'Green snack for big fishy!' She giggled. The dino-fish gobbled it down in one. Then Sami leaned down and gave him a big kiss right on the end of his nose. I could swear that giant monster fish blushed.

Frankie jumped from Pradeep's hand back into the water and led the dino-fish out of the way so that Dr McDoom could start the boat again and pull out.

She waved to us as she steered the motorboat towards the barrier where the reservoir met the river. She circled a couple times to pick up speed and then aimed for a launch ramp off to the side, and with a final gun of the engine . . . she jumped. The motorboat cleared the land barrier and she splashed down in the river on the other side.

'That was pretty cool driving for a non-evil scientist,' I said.

Frankie led the dino-fish in a wide arc towards the barrier to pick up speed. At the last second he stopped, while the dino-fish leaped up and out of the water. It landed in the river just behind Dr McDoom's boat, waved its tail at us and then disappeared into the water.

Frankie sped back over to us and I scooped him back up in his water bottle. 'Well done, Frankie,' I said.

As the hum of the motorboat died away we saw the dino-fish leap out of the river in a back flip. His eyes flashed bright green as he hit the water again.

Pradeep and I shared a look. 'I guess Mark was right,' I said. 'There's a little zombie in that dino-fish after all.'

'Bye-bye big fishy!' Sami yawned as we walked back towards our bikes to meet Mrs Kumar. Pradeep bent down and I boosted Sami up so she could have a piggyback.

'I guess being chased by a genetically engineered prehistoric fish in a swimming pool, helping to rescue a drowning evil kitten, fooling an entire audience of press and scientists *and* doing a zombified fish-to-cave-drawing translation session can really take it out of a toddler,' I said, as Sami's eyes fluttered closed.

'And a zombie goldfish,' Pradeep added, pointing to Frankie, whose snores were creating bubbles in his water bottle.

'They both definitely deserve a nap!' I whispered.

'You're right,' Pradeep replied. '*Just in case.*'

I smiled. 'After all. You never know what evil plan might be lurking just around the corner . . .'

MY BIG FAT ZOMBIE GOLDFISH

MO O'HARA

THIS FISH JUST GOT NASTY!

When Tom's big brother dunks Frankie the goldfish into toxic green gunge, Tom zaps the fish with a battery to bring him back to life! But there's something weird about the new Frankie – he's now a BIG FAT ZOMBIE GOLDFISH with hypnotic powers . . . and he's out for revenge.

MY BIG FAT ZOMBIE GOLDFISH

THE SEAQUEL

MO O'HARA

HE'S BACK . . .
AND BADDER THAN EVER!

Frankie is a BIG FAT ZOMBIE GOLDFISH with hypnotic powers and a mind of his own. When his owner Tom takes him on a trip to the seaside, he finds himself in a stand-off with a Super Zombie Eel – has the fierce fish finally met his match? In the second story, all eyes are on Frankie as he takes on a starring role in the school play!

MY BIG FAT ZOMBIE GOLDFISH

FINS OF FURY

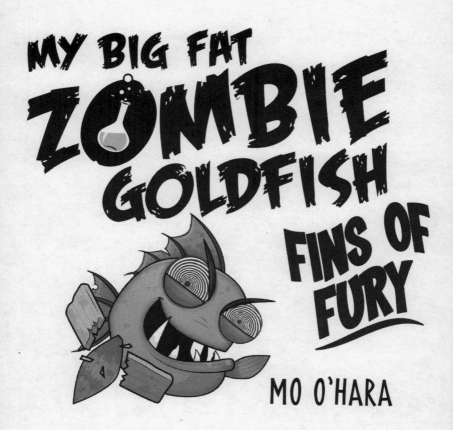

MO O'HARA

FRANKIE'S BACK, AND THIS TIME IT'S PERSONAL!

Frankie is a BIG FAT ZOMBIE GOLDFISH with hypnotic powers. When his owner Tom takes him camping, something fishy starts going on. Could the zombie fish finally have met his match? In story two, Frankie's been kidnapped! Can Tom rescue his fishy friend before it's too late?

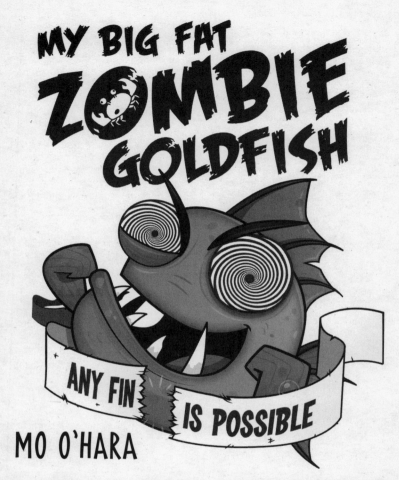

MY BIG FAT ZOMBIE GOLDFISH

ANY FIN IS POSSIBLE

MO O'HARA

ZOMBIE GOLDFISH. VAMPIRE KITTEN. DOUBLE TROUBLE!

Frankie is a BIG FAT ZOMBIE GOLDFISH. When his owner, Tom, takes him to a museum sleepover, history really does come to life. Can Frankie avoid becoming a mummified-kitty snack?

In story two, it's sports day! Can Frankie stop Tom's evil scientist big brother and pet vampire kitten from cheating to bring home the gold?

MY BIG FAT ZOMBIE GOLDFISH
LIVE AND LET SWIM

MO O'HARA

MY NAME'S GOLDFISH.
ZOMBIE GOLDFISH

Frankie, the world's only BIG FAT ZOMBIE GOLDFISH, ends up swimming for his life when his owner, Tom, takes him to an aquarium. Can Frankie defeat a vampire kitten, sharks and a very hungry psychic octopus? In story two, TV show *My Pet's Got Talent* has come to town. But someone is stealing all the pets' amazing abilities. Can Frankie stop the thief without revealing his secret zombie skills?

WWW.GOBSTOPPERBOOKS.COM

VISIT THE GOBSTOPPERS WEBSITE FOR

AUTHOR NEWS · BONUS CONTENT
VIDEOS · GAMES · PRIZES ...

AND MORE!